IN SEARCH OF TWILIGHT

IN SEARCH OF TWILIGHT

Colleen L. Reece

Thorndike Press • Chivers Press
Thorndike, Maine USA   Bath, England

This Large Print edition is published by Thorndike Press, USA and by Chivers Press, England.

Published in 1999 in the U.S. by arrangement with Colleen L. Reece.

Published in 1999 in the U.K. by arrangement with the author.

U.S. Hardcover 0-7862-1872-X (Candlelight Series Edition)
U.K. Hardcover 0-7540-3760-6 (Chivers Large Print)

The text of this Large Print edition is unabridged.
Other aspects of the book may vary from the original edition.

Set in 16 pt. Plantin by Rick Gundberg.

Printed in the United States on permanent paper.

British Library Cataloguing in Publication Data available

Library of Congress Cataloging in Publication Data

Reece, Colleen L.
   In search of twilight / Colleen L. Reece.
      p. (large print) ; cm.
   ISBN 0-7862-1872-X (lg. print : hc : alk paper)
   1. Large type books. I. Title.
   [PS3568.E364615 1999]
   813′.54—dc21   99-11205

IN SEARCH OF TWILIGHT

Chapter 1

"Beggin' your pardon, miss, but are you ill?"

The friendly concern in the weather-beaten face of the questioner penetrated the numbness enveloping Twilight Trevor. With a visible effort she brought her thoughts back to the present, smiling wanly.

"No, thank you."

"You look kind of peaked. I've been keepin' an eye on you ever since we left Chelan. Sure you're okay?"

"I'm fine." The flat response discouraged further conversation. With a keen glance the man tipped his worn cowboy hat and moved away.

Twilight's face flushed. She knew she had been rude, but right now, talking with anyone, even someone as nice as the man seemed to be, would be too much to bear. Yet she was sorry she had been so abrupt. He had only been trying to help.

Help! She laughed bitterly to herself. What was she doing here, anyway? The waves lapping the sides of the *Lady of the Lake* were no stronger than the waves of misery washing over her. Clutching her coat tightly against the nippy breeze, she answered her own question. What else could she have done? For a moment the shoreline of Lake Chelan receded, replaced by pale gold walls of her and Jenny's Seattle apartment. Jenny! She closed her eyes against the fresh stab of pain, trying to shut out memories that seared into her very soul.

I can't think of it now, Twilight thought. When I get to Aunt Lucy I'll tell her the whole thing. It's the only honest way to go. Maybe she can help me think clearly.

Once her decision was made, Twilight felt better. Squaring her shoulders and lifting her proud Trevor chin, she left the railing and went back inside. The kindly man was sitting alone and on impulse she went across to him. "May I join you?"

A warm smile crossed his rugged features. "Glad to have you, miss."

Twilight shook her head. "Not miss" — she hesitated — "I'm Lucy Trevor's niece . . . Angelica." It's not a lie, she assured herself. Angelica is my middle name.

Her companion didn't seem to notice the slight hesitation but held out a brown, workworn hand of welcome.

"Mightly glad to meet you, Miss Angelica.

Everyone up and down the lake knows Lucy. She's a fine person." There was a tremor in his voice, but he hastily added, "I'm Jingles Jacobsen." Sensing her involuntary start at the unusual name, he smiled.

"My real name's Jake, but only one person ever calls me that." He waved out the window. "Hard to believe you've come almost fifty miles up Lake Chelan, isn't it? Chelan's an Indian word for deep water. She's a grand old lake." There was affection and pride in his voice. Twilight didn't have the heart to tell him she had been so absorbed in her own thoughts she had scarcely noticed. Now she gazed out the window. They were coming into shore, where a small cluster of buildings were grouped near the landing. "Is that the town?"

Jingles laughed again. "Stehekin isn't a town and never has been. That's Stehekin Landing, the National Park Service Lodge, Information Center, and so on. Stehekin itself refers to the private community, river, and valley. Must be your first trip here."

"It is. I wondered how to pronounce it. Steh-he-kin . . . is that right? Is it an Indian word too?"

"Sure is. It means the way through."

"The way through." She repeated it slowly, a shadow falling across the purple eyes, then

9

added almost to herself, "I wonder if it will be for me."

Jingles wisely ignored her wistful comment, gathering up her luggage. If he was surprised by the number of pieces he said nothing until they had disembarked.

"There's your Aunt Lucy." An ancient jeep was just pulling up. Shaking hands again, he looked directly into the girl's eyes. "There's another Indian word we use a lot up here — *tillicum*. It means good friend. If you ever need anything, just holler for Jingles." His gruff sincerity almost broke Twilight's composure. She gripped the calloused hand hard and promised, "I will." Blinking back tears, she ran to the jeep, forestalling Aunt Lucy's ready greeting.

"Here's your very own niece Angelica," she called. Aunt Lucy didn't so much as bat an eye at the unused name, but held out her arms. "I'm so glad you're here . . . Angelica."

Twilight flew into the welcoming embrace, then pulled back as her eyes fell on the long white cast covering her aunt's left leg from toes to knee.

"Oh, that! It's nothing. Slipped on my steps like a crazy loon."

"Shouldn't you be in the hospital?" Twilight demanded.

"I was, but the Chelan doctor said I was too

ornery to keep! I'm all right." She raised her voice, calling to Jingles, "How about sending Tommy over to help with the chores tonight? Frank Wilson did them while I was gone but he's got his own hands full. Tommy can earn a bit for that bike he's been saving for."

"Sure thing." Jingles's reply was hearty. "What with Miss Angelica taking over your school, she'll sure be too busy to help much."

Before Twilight could protest her aunt snapped, "Don't stand there with your mouth open, get in." Her crustiness was tempered by the twinkle in her blue eyes.

"Blabbermouth!" she accused the grinning Jingles. "I hadn't told her yet." With a jerk she put the jeep in reverse, spun around, and headed away from the landing. "I'll tell you about it after supper," she relented, as the wide-eyed Twilight watched her maneuver the jeep onto the main valley road. Chuckling at her expression, Aunt Lucy said, "Good thing it was my left leg. Couldn't drive if it had been the right."

Aunt Lucy's cottage was nestled in a clump of trees starting to turn color from the late September weather. Small, but perfectly proportioned, it looked like heaven to the tired girl. The room her aunt showed her wasn't much bigger than the closet of Twilight's Seattle apartment, but the ruffled curtains, natural pine walls and braided rug on the floor held out open arms of welcome. It was too much for Twilight's frayed nerves. She dropped to the spotless white chenille spread and burst into tears.

In spite of the cast Aunt Lucy wasted no time. In moments she had the girl's head in her lap. "You may as well tell me," she advised quietly. "You won't rest until you do."

Her heart ached for the girl, lovely in face and spirit as her beautiful name. The great purple eyes were like pansies drenched with rain, with shadows that should not have been there in one so young. Only twenty-one, Twilight had already experienced more than her share of tragedy. She had been just eighteen, her sister Jenny fifteen, when their beloved parents were killed in a plane crash. To add to the mess, while their father had been a wonderful parent and brother, he had not been a businessman. After expenses were paid, very little was left. Twilight was determined to drop out of college to support Jenny and herself, but Aunt Lucy stepped in. She would have none of it.

"You girls are both too intelligent not to finish school," she insisted. "Twilight, you are to stay in college. I have enough to put you both through, and you can't depend on

12

finding work without an education. You won't be able to be extravagant, but there will be enough." Over their protests she installed the girls in a second-floor apartment, roomy but old-fashioned, in one of her friend's homes. She asked only that they consult the Matthewsons if they needed anything.

Both girls determined to repay her by excelling in their studies. Twilight surpassed Jenny, graduating from college with honors just the past June, but Jenny had also graduated from high school in the top five per cent of her class and was enrolled at the University of Washington in pre-nursing.

A frown crossed Aunt Lucy's face. She was a little worried about Jenny. The last time she had been in Seattle the girl didn't look well. Under the same wealth of rich brown hair that Twilight possessed, Jenny's big brown eyes looked lost in her small white face. I better check on her, Aunt Lucy decided. But right now it was Twilight who needed attention.

The girl's sobs had subsided somewhat and she could talk coherently. Gradually the story came out, part of which Aunt Lucy knew. There was anger, bitterness, and hurt mingled, but most of all, hopelessness. Aunt Lucy had never seen Twilight so distraught.

Jefferson Stone was a clean-cut, fine young man doing graduate work in forestry at the

University of Washington when he and Twilight met six months ago. If ever there had been a case of love at first sight, theirs was it. From the moment they were introduced at a mutual friend's party, they had spent all their free time together.

Twilight with her purple eyes and evening shades of clothing she wore so often, amethyst, lilac, gray, purple; Jeff, tall, dark, gray-eyed, a tower of strength. Heads turned wherever they went. Twilight found herself leaning on him, for the first time in her life depending on someone else's presence for her happiness. His very goodness and understanding undermined her firm determination to stay away from romance until Jenny finished her R.N. training and had her degree.

"He said Jenny was part of me, without her I would be incomplete. If we married her home would be with us for as long as she wanted it that way. He loved her like a sister." There was a painful twist to her words. "That's why I didn't sign a teaching contract for this fall. Jeff isn't sure where he will be going. He has had several offers, money is no problem. He felt it might be good for me to be home for a while and have more time for Jenny, and for him." A soft blush mantled her cheek, replaced by a fresh burst of tears.

Aunt Lucy held her closely, almost afraid to

hear what was coming. She had been impressed with Jeff. He was the only modern young man she had seen whom she felt was good enough for such a special person as Twilight. The rest of the story was almost unbelievable.

Twilight had been wearing Jeff's ring for about a month when it happened. He had ordered an amethyst set in tiny diamonds, to "match her," he said. He seemed to almost worship her, putting her on a pedestal. "Then just a few nights ago . . ." Twilight's voice failed, but she bravely took up the story. One of her classes was canceled, so she arrived home earlier than usual. Hearing voices from the living room, she stepped to the doorway to call out gaily. Her greeting died on her lips. In the middle of the room stood Jeff, arms tightly clasped about Jenny. His face was white. "We've got to tell her!"

"I can't," Jenny sobbed. "It will kill her!"

Twilight's involuntary gasp froze the two in their places as they looked up and saw her white face. Then she was running, down, down, out to the street and a bus just pulling away. With a final burst of speed she made the bus, not caring what the destination might be. Looking back she saw Jeff frantically running down the street, beckoning to her.

"I rode to the end of the line, got off, and

went to a hotel," she finished dully. "Nothing he could say would erase what I'd seen. No wonder he was so anxious for her to live with us! I just wouldn't have dreamed he would be interested in an eighteen-year-old girl; he's older, you know. He was in the service before college, so he's almost thirty. How could there be any explanation? The next day after calling both the apartment and the Matthewsons to make sure no one was home, I slipped in, packed as much as I dared take time for, and left my ring in a box addressed to Jeff. I didn't know what to do, so here I am." There was utter defeat in her voice as she sat up and made a futile attempt to smooth down her hair.

"I suppose I should have stayed and faced them, but Aunt Lucy, I just couldn't! Jeff and Jenny, the two people I care most for in the whole world! I don't ever want to see them again. That's why when I told Jingles who I was I said Angelica."

Aunt Lucy sat motionless. Twilight's story was incredible. Yet, what other explanation was there? She shook her head slowly.

"Something doesn't quite fit. I still think there has to be more to it than you realize. Neither Jeff nor Jenny are dishonorable. If they had fallen in love I believe they would have come to you and admitted it. I can't see that either of them would hurt you in any way."

For a moment hope flickered in Twilight's eyes. "I've told myself that over and over. I just can't seem to get my bearings. You're the only person I could even tell. I've never felt so crushed and humiliated before. Maybe it's been good for me. Maybe I expected happiness too much."

"Don't ever say that!" her aunt reproved sharply. "Remember what Stehekin means — the way through. If any place on earth can help you sort things out, this is it. As much as you can, put it aside for a while. Given time, things have a way of working themselves out. In the meantime, I can smell our dinner burning. We've had enough seriousness on empty stomachs. You know, Twilight, nothing ever seems so bad as on an empty stomach or in the middle of the night."

She rose awkwardly and started for the door. "Better hurry. I put that stew on before I went to meet you." The door banged behind her. Twilight smiled tremulously. Aunt Lucy's reaction to her miserable story had done more than all her own philosophizing. For the first time since leaving Seattle she felt alive again. While the pain was still fresh, her own youthful optimism was beginning to bounce back. There was a dull ache within,

but there was also a tiny spark refusing to die.
Could Aunt Lucy be right? Would Stehekin
show her the way through?

Chapter 2

Twilight was amazed to find herself asking for seconds on Aunt Lucy's delicious stew, homemade bread, and applesauce. She had been sure she wouldn't be able to swallow a mouthful.

"You reckoned without all the fresh air." Aunt Lucy chuckled, seeing the slight uptilt of the girl's mouth. "Good hot food can certainly make a difference in a person's attitude. Nothing looks worse than a picked-chicken miserable person."

Twilight had to nod agreement. Over her aunt's protest she cleared the table, did up the few dishes, and put them away. "I was surprised to find you have electricity way up here," she commented, noting the shiny faucets and hot water.

Aunt Lucy bristled. "There's lots of things people on the outside don't know." A slight resentment edged her tone.

"Just because some of us choose to live away from the world of cities and crime most people call civilization is no reason for us to be thought of as a bunch of hicks, or savages! Nothing could be further from the truth. This is a big country. It takes big people to live here. Many have come and gone away complaining of the loneliness and harshness of the winters. They failed to see what Stehekin really is. It can bring out unsuspected depths of character. If you stay, and I hope you will, Twilight, you'll meet people who have encountered problems and come through with flying colors. That doesn't mean this is a haven for runaways. A lot of us are living here because we chose to make it our home. Others were born here, went away, and came back. But whatever the reason, it's from choice.

"Stehekin. The way through. It's more than just a trite phrase or a passage through the mountains. It has come to mean a challenge, a rewarding way of life, simple and uncluttered by too much civilization."

Twilight remained silent, gazing into the lazy fire column rising in the blackened fireplace. Aunt Lucy's words had touched her deeply, and for the first time she felt it right to ask, "Why did you come?"

It was a question she and Jenny had asked each other over the years, but something held it back. Now, with her own defenses down, Twilight felt she had to know.

Aunt Lucy's face softened, her hands lying idly in her aproned lap. They were workworn hands, calloused, rough, but in them Twilight suddenly saw beauty. They were hands like those of Jingles, useful, loving hands. Rosy flames from the burning log cast grotesque patterns on Aunt Lucy's propped up white cast, but her face was in shadow.

"It was long ago. I'd grown up without much but by hard work and determination achieved what I then thought of as success. Although still young in years, I was given the position of associate professor at the U. It was the same old story. I was forced to choose between home and career. Things were different then, and my childhood sweetheart was strongly opposed to a working wife and mother.

"We quarreled. Within a week I realized what a bitter mistake I'd made, but was too proud to admit it. Achingly in love, miserable, yet I couldn't say I was wrong. A few months later he married on the rebound, a woman totally unworthy of him. He did everything he knew how to make it work, but in a few years she drifted away, and was later killed in a car accident, along with her second husband. There was only one son. I kept track of them all those years of financial success, so empty inside.

"Leaving Seattle, my former fiance and his son came here and started a guide service into the mountains. I had written after Lucile's death expressing sympathy, but received no answer. Yet I felt at least partly to blame for his unhappy life. Taking the bit in my teeth, I resigned my professorship, and with fear and trembling applied for the Stehekin one-room school job, signing my name simply L. Trevor. It was harder then to get a teacher up here than now. I understand the last time they needed one, nearly a hundred applications were received! Anyway, I was afraid they wouldn't consider a woman, so I conveniently left that fact out of my letter of application." She paused to laugh reminiscently.

"In spite of the valley chivalry I was so afraid they wouldn't even consider a woman! The teacher not only has all eight grades in the one-room school, but shovels snow and gets the firewood!

"Undaunted, I arrived at Stehekin Landing scared to death, a signed contract to prove my right to be here, and determined to make good. After the first gasp of disapproval, I was accepted. Sometimes I was only a few jumps ahead of my students with their lovable ways and atrocious practical jokes, but I did it. I taught for several years and had my little home built. I retired a year ago. However, the young man who replaced me, and who was doing an excellent job, was called home because of his father's illness. They asked me to substitute until a replacement was found. The end of September is a bad time to find a good teacher. By then the good ones have either found jobs or become established in other lines of work. I agreed to help out."

Light began to glimmer and Twilight said suspiciously, "And?"

Her aunt squirmed. "Well, everything was fine until I broke my leg. Then I got your note and just happened to mention . . ." Her voice trailed off.

Twilight was aghast. "Aunt Lucy, you didn't!"

"I did too," she said defensively. "After all, you were top of your class."

"I? Teach all eight grades in one room? I couldn't teach and they wouldn't learn!"

Her aunt's self-consciousness fled. "Of course you can, Twilight, at least until they find a suitable teacher." Her voice sparkled with enthusiasm. "I made it a point to see your student-teaching reviews. I still have some pull at the U! You'll be fine. Twilight, nowhere else could you find the experience you can get here. These people are among the finest on earth and they need you. . . . I do too." The note of sadness accomplished what persuasion could not have done.

"I'll try," Twilight promised. "I guess as long as I'm here, the least I can do is help out. But it's only until they find someone else!" she warned, seeing the glint in her aunt's eye.

"Of course," her aunt said meekly. "You won't regret it, Twilight."

The fragile moment was shattered by a thunderous knock followed by the precipitate entrance of a towheaded boy with a gorgeous collie dog.

"Down, Wolf," Aunt Lucy commanded as the big dog flung himself across the room to Twilight, but with a delighted croon the girl held our her hands.

"What a beautiful creature!" she cried, stroking the silky fur and winning the heart of her first pupil at the same time.

"Tommy," Aunt Lucy introduced, "this is your new substitute teacher, Miss Angelica."

"Oh, boy," Tommy exploded, watching the beautiful girl stroke his dog while a broad grin split the freckled face. "Wait till I spread the word!"

His wholehearted approval boosted Twilight's shaken ego. Her spirits lifted. If all her students were like Tommy, teaching would be a pleasure. She studied him more closely as Aunt Lucy gave instructions on what he was to do. About ten, wiry yet giving the appearance of strength, the boy looked like someone Twilight knew.

Puzzled, she shook her head. She couldn't place him. After he had gone she asked Aunt Lucy, "Who are Tommy's parents? He looks familiar to me but I don't know him."

"His parents are both dead. Tommy's father was an Air Force pilot and was killed while testing a new design of plane. The shock was too much and the mother died shortly after. About two years ago Tommy's grandfather brought him and his little sister Honey here. She's six now."

Aunt Lucy looked directly at Twilight.

"Tommy is the spitting image of his grandfather when he was that age."

"You mean . . . ?"

"Yes, Tommy's grandfather was once my fiance, and is the man you met on the boat, Jake Jacobsen. Tommy and Honey are the grandchildren I could have had if I hadn't been so stubbornly set on doing things my own way." She was still for so long Twilight wondered if the conversation was over, then she went on.

"The minute I saw Jake after all those years I knew the love of childhood had deepened. I felt he cared too, but I know he won't speak. He feels that if what he had to offer so long ago wasn't enough, then what he is now is much less. I thought my coming would show how the proud, willful girl he once knew had grown up and become a woman. But Jake is the proud one now. He is waiting for me to say I'm sorry. Each day brings me closer to it, but then I think, what if I'm wrong? What if it is too late, what if he doesn't care? It would only embarrass us both."

She grinned at Twilight. "He doesn't know how much I long to just march right out to his horse ranch and guide service and tell him I've come to stay . . . and I may just do it one of these days, too!"

Twilight laughed out loud at the thought of her aunt, cast and all, arriving at the ranch in the dusty jeep and throwing herself into Jingles's arms, but sobered when the woman said, "That's why I don't want you to let false pride separate you and Jeff if there is any reasonable reason for his actions . . . or you and Jenny."

Twilight didn't want to discuss them right then so she asked breathlessly, "How did Jingles get his name?"

A devilish little light sprang to Aunt Lucy's eyes. "From his horse. Yes, he really did! When Jake first started out here he was a real greenhorn. He relied on his hands to set him straight. They liked and respected him but certainly weren't above all type of practical jokes.

"There was one buckskin pony he especially liked to ride. Yet no matter how close to camp the horse was hobbled, the next morning he would invariably be gone. Jake would have to hunt him down, and was amazed to find he was still hobbled!

"At last he caught on and saw through their trick. Every night one of the boys would lead the horse away, and let on he had strayed.

"Instead of spoiling their fun by calling the bluff, Jake sent for a long string of jingle bells. He innocently told the outfit he thought it would be a good idea to put jingle bells on his horse, then if it strayed he would hear it. To this day the boys aren't sure whether he caught on and was having the last laugh or if they really fooled him, but the name Jingles stuck."

Remembering the big man's words on the boat ride Twilight said, "He told me only one person ever calls him Jake. That's you, isn't it?"

Aunt Lucy nodded. "Yes, he will always be Jake to me. It brings back memories of happier days, and perhaps dreams of years to come." Quick tears stung Twilight's throat. What a love, to last like that, over the years! Would her feeling for Jeff be so strong?

"You've found your way through, haven't you, Aunt Lucy?"

"Not completely." Her aunt looked out the window, then back. "I've often thought my life was like a tunnel. Many years of dullness away from the fresh air and beauty. Now I'm nearing the end of that underground existence. I can see spring, and summer, winter, and fall ahead. I can see sunshine and laughter. I'm almost to the end, and soon will be able to step out and be free. But maybe I will appreciate it all more because of the gloomy time before.

"Believe me, Twilight, it's a growing thing. You'll find it too, as life itself." The peace in her aunt's voice spilled over.

"Your agreeing to step outside your own misery and help others is the first step. For one thing you'll be kept far too busy to brood. I thought you might like to use the lesson plans I started, at least at first. You'll have enough to do getting acquainted to prepare all the classes you'll need."

Gratefully Twilight nodded. She would need all the help she could get! Yet now that her decision was made a thrill of strong anticipation shot through her. If Aunt Lucy could do it, then so could she!

"When do I start?"

"Today's Saturday. We'll see most of the

folks at church tomorrow and they can pass the word. Why not Monday? That's a good day for beginnings, and the school was closed last week while I was gone."

Twilight gulped. She had secretly hoped for a little more time to get ready, but she lifted her chin in that way she had and said, "That will be fine."

Her aunt's approving glance was reward enough. For her sake Twilight would probably have agreed to walk barefoot through the snow and teach fifty children instead of the ten now enrolled!

"Why don't you go out for a bit?" her aunt asked. "Tommy would be pleased if you go see his work. Besides it's almost 'your time of day.'" Both women smiled, remembering how as a child Twilight had emphatically stated evening was hers. Tossing a warm sweater over her shoulder against the late September chill even though it was only afternoon by her city standards, she walked around the small yard.

In spite of the cold weather there were still small flowers here and there braving the chill. The leaves were beautiful against the green trees, red, yellow, orange. It was so quiet! The silence was almost tangible.

Twilight breathed in great gulps of the fresh air. It was so clean and cold it hurt her lungs;

she could almost taste it. When had she smelled air like that? It reminded her of childhood and camping out. The slight smell of wood smoke brought back days when the four of them had visited various places and slept under the stars. How close they had been then, Dad, Mom, Jenny, and herself! Would she and Jenny ever be close again?

Determinedly she shoved the thought away. Now was not the time to grow morbid. Time would help give her a sense of proportion, a way through the tunnel, as Aunt Lucy had said.

What was that strange grunting sound? Twilight knew Aunt Lucy had a few chickens but she had said nothing about pigs. It didn't quite sound like a pig, but what else could it be? She'd ask Tommy.

Rounding the corner of the small shed next to the cottage, Twilight froze in her tracks. There before her stood a huge black, furry bear. She had come up behind it — evidently the wind was in the other direction — and it wasn't ten feet away. Even as she noted its presence her eyes, now keen with horror, spotted Tommy backed against the wall of the shed. His rifle was out of reach, and Wolf was frantically barking, straining against Tommy's desperate clutch that kept her from attacking the menace. The grunting changed to snarls and suddenly the huge animal started toward the white-faced boy.

Without thinking of the danger involved, Twilight despairingly looked around for something to throw. A brick leftover from chimney repairs was close at hand. Seizing it with both hands, she threw it at the creature with all her might, praying it would find its mark. With a glad cry she saw it hit. The animal hesitated, then with a ferocious roar turned and started directly toward her.

Unable to move, she could only stare fascinated at the baleful eyes glaring hate from the insulted bear. Tommy's hoarse shout, "Run!" released her from her spell. With all her strength she dodged around the corner of the shed, dropping her sweater in her flight. For a moment the bear hesitated over the white object in its path, turning the corner just as Tommy snatched up the rifle. Wolf sprang toward the bear as Twilight tripped over another brick in her flight.

This is the end, she thought, falling to the ground. Faintly she heard three shots, then a great, heavy fur blanket fell across her feet. Mercifully she blacked out, her last cry for help smothered by the weight slowly pressing her into oblivion.

Chapter 3

Somewhere in the darkness, a long way off, someone was calling. "Miss Angel, Miss Angel!" Struggling to free herself from the chains holding her down, Twilight groped for reality. Was she dead? Why was someone calling her an angel? Was this heaven, then? Slowly she remembered Tommy, the bear coming for her, the shots, the darkness.

With a mighty effort she opened her eyes. Something wet was on her face — it was Wolf, licking her in an ecstasy of joy at her being alive.

"I'm not dead!" The fact startled her. Pushing her hair back, she sat up to meet Tommy's anxious gaze.

"Of course you aren't," he assured her, anxiety replaced with his grin. "You just saved my life, that's all. 'Course, you kind of keeled over when you fell and thought the bear had got you."

"The bear!" A fresh wave of fear swept over Twilight. "Where is it?"

Tommy pointed to the great furry blanket

across her feet and legs, pride showing in every line of his small figure.

"Right there. She fell across you when I shot her."

Curiously Twilight looked at the great animal and with Tommy's help removed it from her feet. She shuddered to think how close she had been to a horrible death.

Tommy was all concern. "You'd better get in the house. We'll leave the bear where it is. Grandad will come over and take care of her. How would you like it made into a nice bear rug?"

Controlling a desire to laugh, thinking of the look on her Seattle friends' faces if she took home that giant skin, she quietly told Tommy, "That would be great."

He beamed with pleasure and led her to the house.

Aunt Lucy was just getting into a sweater, before coming out to find out what was happening. Her hands shook as Tommy told the story, heroically giving Twilight credit for saving his life.

"Wait a minute," she denied, "it was you that shot the bear. All I did was throw a brick."

Tommy would have none of her arguments. "If you hadn't thrown the brick I'd have been a goner. My rifle was leaned up too far to reach before she got me. Miss Angel, thanks." His face burned with earnestness. Seeing how touched the boy was, Twilight said no more.

"What a horrible welcome for you to Stehekin!" Aunt Lucy recovered enough to say. "Tommy, heat some milk for cocoa. I think Twilight could stand something warm, and you too. You'll still have time to get home before dark, it's only a half mile."

Twilight didn't know how bad her reaction was going to be until she sank into a chair. All at once the whole thing hit her, and she made a visible effort to control the shaking knees and chattering teeth that followed. For the first time in her life she had been close to death, and a terrible one at that. With shaking hands she gratefully accepted the hot chocolate, which seemed to warm her through and through.

"Are there many bears here?" she asked tremulously, trying to hide her fear.

Tommy answered, a rim of cocoa around his mouth.

"Yes, but it's only lately we have had trouble with them. They used to come down to the landing and get the garbage. They didn't bother anybody and no one bothered them. This summer we've had a bunch of crazy tourists up here feeding them and

34

teasing them. Now the bears expect trouble from us. Most of it is closer to the landing. Miss Angel, you'll have to learn to shoot."

"Me?" she gasped ungrammatically, startled for a moment by his confidence in her.

"Sure, I'll teach you. It's a half mile from here to school, but in the opposite direction from me. If you want, I can teach you to drive the jeep, too."

"Just a minute, young man," Aunt Lucy put in. "You're too young to be in that jeep on the main country road down the valley. It's one thing to drive on your grandad's place, but the road is something else."

"Aw shucks," the boy murmured, red tingeing his clear brown skin. "I know how plenty good."

Twilight sensed an argument of long standing.

"Since it's such nice weather I'll walk. By the time it snows and I need the jeep, they will have another teacher." She failed to catch the exchange of looks between Tommy and her aunt. If she had seen Tommy's face just then she would have noticed the expression that said as clearly as words, Oh yeah?

Tommy jumped up. "Come on, Wolf. We've got to get home." He paused in the doorway. "Good night, Aunt Lucy. Good night, Miss Angel. See you at church tomorrow."

Aunt Lucy laughed as the door shut behind him and his merry whistle echoed back through the growing dusk.

"You've been named, Twilight. No one in Stehekin will ever call you Miss Angelica now. Tommy's shortened version will be picked up immediately."

"I don't deserve it." She shook her head. "We both know who the real hero was. I was so frozen I couldn't even think, but when that bear started for Tommy . . ." Her voice broke in a sob.

"You did the best you knew how," her aunt finished. "Thank God for that."

Twilight looked curiously at Aunt Lucy. "You really believe God interferes?"

"Of course." Her aunt looked surprised at the question. "If He cared enough to make us, then surely He cares enough to be concerned when we need Him, or when we call on Him for help."

"I think you must be right," Twilight replied slowly. She told her aunt how when she threw the brick she prayed it would stop the bear. Tears glistened in Aunt Lucy's eyes.

"Twilight, Stehekin is already taking hold of you. I don't want to preach but I will tell you one thing I hope you never forget. The

36

only reason we don't get God's help oftener is because we forget to ask . . . and to trust that it will be answered." She poked the dying fire until a shower of sparks flared up the chimney.

"If it hadn't been for my faith throughout the years I couldn't have kept going. Neither could Jingles, or many of the others here. Out here we are more dependent on Him, and on each other. There's less of what man has accomplished, maybe that makes it easier for us to see His work. I only know that there is peace from any trouble available — if we will reach out and take it."

Long after her aunt was asleep that night Twilight shivered in the darkness, huddled under many homemade quilts on her bed. For the first time since leaving Seattle she forced herself to go back over every detail, ending with her experience that afternoon.

Her aunt's words came back to her as she tossed and turned restlessly.

"Peace from any trouble available . . . reach out."

Shyly she whispered, "Please, give me peace and help me help the students." Brief, but she felt better afterward, and in a few moments was sound asleep, lulled by the whispering of the giant pines outside her window.

A bright ray of sunshine woke her early the next morning, even before Aunt Lucy was up. For a moment all the doubts and fears swept over her, but resolutely she put them aside. Again her aunt's words came back to her, "Ask . . . then trust." She had asked, now she must learn to trust, and wait. She felt more at peace with herself this morning. Was it a result of the little prayer?

Smiling to herself, she quietly slipped from bed and tiptoed to the kitchen. No reason why she couldn't have breakfast ready when her aunt awakened. She had no idea what time church was, but perhaps it would be early.

Seven thirty. She glanced at the clock thinking, I wonder if Jenny is up now? Quickly thrusting aside the idea, she deftly prepared a good breakfast from the food she found on hand. Orange juice, scrambled eggs, freshly toasted homemade bread. The fragrance wafted to her aunt's room and within moments her beaming face appeared at the doorway. She was wrapped in a warm robe, her cast clumping along.

"What's going on in my kitchen?" she pretended to growl.

"Who's afraid of the big, bad wolf?" Twilight defied her. "Here, sit down. Breakfast is all ready."

"Pretty good maid service, I'd say," Aunt Lucy announced a little later. They had eaten every scrap Twilight had prepared. Twilight's delighted laugh trilled out like silver bells. It was good to be needed.

"What time is church? Do you have a regular minister?"

"It is ten o'clock. The minister from one of the other small lake towns comes in, often flies. We are interdenominational. We don't put a brand on the church. I think you will find it quite interesting, Twilight. Services are held in the old Golden West Lodge, a large frame building just a little way from the Park Information Office. You can look right down through the trees to Lake Chelan from the front porch."

How right she was, Twilight thought later as she and her aunt stepped to the porch of the Golden West Lodge. The lake was intensely blue through the trees, and faithfully reflected in its shining expanse the fall coloring touching the birches on the shores. The yellow leaves and white bark reflection made it difficult to realize where the shore left off and image began.

Twilight had wondered how her aunt could make it up the rather steep incline from the landing to the lodge, but she reckoned without the useful little jeep. It landed them right near the door and because of Aunt Lucy's leg, they left it parked there.

The service was well attended. Twilight was impressed by the simplicity, and by the many valley folk she met. Her head was whirling from trying to remember "who belonged to whom." When the regular service was over, Jingles stood and held up a big hand.

"Before we go, I want to introduce you to someone. Most of you may have met her, but I doubt you know just what she has done for us already." He went on to tell in glowing terms, evidently amplified by Tommy, how "Miss Angel" had saved his grandson's life. He made little of Tommy's part in the affair — boys were expected to be able to shoot — but praised Twilight highly for her unorthodox way of halting the bear's rush toward the child. Unashamed tears stood in his eyes as he stood with a big hand on Tommy's shoulder, the other resting lightly on the golden curls of the little six-year-old Honey.

"I guess all of you know what it would have meant to me if she hadn't been there," he said simply. "She's going to help out with our kids at school." He paused to look directly at the young people in the congregation.

"If I hear of any shenanigans down there, someone will be answering to me personally!"

Even the most mischievous boy quelled under his look. There would be no trouble at the school, Jingles had made sure of that. It was the only way he knew to say thank you for what Twilight had done.

Declining several invitations to dinner, Aunt Lucy and Twilight drove quietly home from church. Each had a lot to think about; there was also much to do. After dinner they gathered together Aunt Lucy's lesson plans and the curly white head and shining brown one pored over them together.

"Actually, you're lucky," Aunt Lucy told Twilight. "Although it's an all eight-grade school, this year there are no second or seventh graders. That means you only have about six grades, seven classes each, or forty-two units to teach."

Twilight's gasp stopped her. "Forty-two? In one day?"

Aunt Lucy smiled. "It isn't as bad as seven times eight grades, or the fifty-six I started with!" She relented a bit. "Look, it isn't all that bad." She showed Twilight the basic subjects: Reading, Writing, Spelling, they could be grouped together. Arithmetic. Social Studies. Health and Science could be taught together. By the time they had finished, Twilight's head was in a whirl. Yet she realized that without Aunt Lucy's careful preparation she would have been defeated before even starting.

"The older ones hear the little ones recite," Aunt Lucy said. "It not only helps them review, but gives them a feeling of usefulness." The long, golden afternoon hours sped by, and by suppertime Twilight felt she had just taken a crash memory course. Her heart pounded at the thought of the first day, yet something deep within had jelled into a solid determination to do it, and do it well.

After supper they sat on the tiny porch until it grew too cold for comfort, then once again curled up in front of the fireplace. Twilight had already realized the fireplace was the heart of Aunt Lucy's home, especially now with colder weather coming on. There was a brisk chill in the air.

"This is my favorite time of day, too," Aunt Lucy confided. "It's a time of peace, of ending the day quietly. I often feel sorry for those in the city who wait until evening hours for their dinner." Twilight was already growing accustomed to the valley usage of "breakfast," "dinner," and "supper" rather than "breakfast," "lunch," and "dinner" as used in town.

"The noon meal has to be more than a little lunch for hard-working people," her aunt told her. "When folks spend the twilight hours eating they miss the best part of the day. Your folks felt that way too, that's why they named you Twilight. I remember how your mother hoped you would be born then, and you were. Your big eyes opened and they were the purple-blue of the evening haze on distant mountains. 'Twilight,' your mother whispered, and Twilight you became." Her voice was gentle, soothing, full of love.

"I'm glad you told me," the girl whispered, unwilling to break the moment of perfect harmony between them. "I remember now that when I was small Mother told me the same thing, but I had forgotten. Oh, Aunt Lucy, I'm glad I came!"

Her wise aunt smiled. She could have said "I told you so," pointing out that already time was beginning to wear down the problems that only yesterday had seemed insurmountable to Twilight. But it wasn't for her to do. While she could show the way, Twilight must take the path for herself. She must find her own way through. Aunt Lucy had no fear but what she would find it, and sooner than Twilight might think. The quiet stillness of Stehekin was beginning its work, and a solid foundation was being formed for the peace that would come.

Chapter 4

When the door slammed behind Twilight, it released the frozen state Jefferson Stone and Jenny had gone into at the sound of her gasp. With a muttered exclamation Jeff tore himself free from Jenny's automatic clutch of dismay and bounded through the door and down the stairs.

"Wait, Twilight," he called out, but only a glimpse of her white, set face was visible as the bus pulled away from the curb. Jeff stood on the sidewalk, staring after the departing vehicle, then slowly, with shoulders slumped, walked back up the stairs to the girls' apartment. Jenny, who had been christened Jennet, was huddled in a low chair, sobbing her heart out. Anger at Twilight mingled with pity hoarsened Jeff's voice as he crossed to her.

"Don't," he pleaded, stroking the soft hair. "Don't cry, Jenny." Tenderness filled him as he looked down at her, such a little girl in so many ways. He had always wanted a younger sister and when Twilight introduced him to

Jenny, he had been immediately drawn to the pale face and haunting brown eyes. He thought Twilight knew how he felt. How could she have misunderstood?

"Oh, Jeff," Jenny cried, "what are we going to do? How could she look at us like that, as if she hated us both?" The pain in her voice increased the deadly anger beginning to grow within Jeff. Trust was the basis of the kind of love he and Twilight had shared. Had shared, he thought bitterly. She hadn't even given them time to explain.

"She should have known we wouldn't be dishonorable," he told Jenny roughly, emotion threatening to spill over. "She should have trusted us enough to at least find out why we were here."

The hopelessness in his tone touched through Jenny's own grief. Wide-eyed, she stared at the man she loved as a brother and realization hit her.

"It's my fault." There was deadness in the quavering voice. "I wish I were dead! I'd rather be dead than hurt Twilight."

Jeff wheeled from the window where he had turned. "Stop that!" he commanded sharply. "Twilight should know us well enough to give us the benefit of the doubt. Besides, how could you have done anything different? That doctor's report was enough to make anyone upset. I'm glad that you trusted me enough to come to me with it. I'm only sorry that now, when you need her more than any other time in your life, she should be off somewhere. Do you have any idea where she might have gone? Can we find her?"

A new horror sprang to Jenny's eyes. "You mean she might not come back? Oh, Jeff, surely she'll be back home this evening!" Her plea for help was so much like the cry of a child that Jeff winced. He would give anything to spare Jenny what might lie ahead. But who knew where Twilight might have gone? How could they find her? She had dozens of friends, any one of whom she might seek out. Or in her hurt, shocked state at what she thought she had seen, would she find a place to literally bury herself for a while?

With a confidence far greater than he actually felt he assured Jenny, "Of course. She will probably be home tonight." Yet the huskiness in his voice belied the words. Jenny said no more, but he could see she wasn't any more convinced than he himself was.

Throughout the long afternoon and evening hours they waited, Jeff and Jenny, waiting for Twilight to return. Twilight, who they loved more than life itself. Twilight, with her beauty, her understanding, her love.

I should have boarded that bus and made

her listen, Jeff thought dully. I should have shaken some sense into her. Jenny needs her so much!

I need her, Jenny thought. If only Twilight would come! Why was I so weak? When Jeff listened to what the doctor told me and held out his arms, it was like a refuge. But why did I run to him? If Twilight only knew! If only she knew!

It became apparent as the evening lengthened that Twilight was not going to return that night. Finally Jeff left, after telling Mrs. Matthewson Jenny wasn't feeling well and Twilight had to be gone that night. The good woman bustled about and quickly prepared a tray for Jenny, appetizing as her good cookery demanded, but Jenny only wanly picked at it.

"Thanks, Mrs. Matthewson, but I just don't feel like eating," she said, unwilling to hurt her landlady's feelings by lack of interest in the dainty meal. When she had gone Jenny bundled into a warm robe and curled up on the couch by the window.

Tomorrow, she thought. Twilight will come tomorrow. She has no clothes with her. At last she fell into a troubled sleep and woke shivering in the chill autumn air. It was a gray day in Seattle, and the fog and rain seemed to depress Jenny even further. Jeff called early and came over as soon as he finished an exam he hadn't dared miss. It was the last of job-application testing, crucial to his future. He didn't dare cut the appointment — it could mean his whole career. He had taken the precaution to check outside Jenny's door when he came in. Perhaps there would be a note. But there was nothing.

Again, anger filled him, mingled with despair. If she couldn't have trusted him, she might have had a little faith in her sister. Hadn't she seen the plea for help in the thin, white face, the big brown eyes? How could she think — his thought refused to finish the sentence.

I don't care if I ever find her, he told himself, even as deep inside a voice whispered, You don't mean that. Steeling himself he added, I only wish I could find her for Jenny's sake. Jenny, who was facing an unknown future. Jenny, the sweet, the shy. Thank God she had turned eighteen. She could sign the necessary papers herself.

His spirit groaned within him. Why couldn't he do more? But as he strode up the stairs he forced a cheerful whistle. Mustn't let Jenny know how worried he was. She had another doctor's appointment this afternoon and it was vitally important she be as calm as possible. Yet when he faced the slim girl he knew she was in turmoil. The white hands were trembling, there were blue shadows beneath the brown eyes, her whole figure drooped.

"She hasn't come," Jenny said, verging on tears. "I waited, and waited —" Her outflung hand indicated the couch where she had stayed all night waiting for her sister.

"Now, Jenny," Jeff reassured the girl. "She probably went somewhere and spent the night in the hotel. To be fair, it probably did look to her as though we had been what my old grandmother called 'carryin' on.' " He was rewarded by a slight smile and continued in the forced cheerful way. "She will have had time to think things over and by evening should be right back here."

"But what if she isn't, Jeff? My surgery is on Monday."

"Monday! Do you think Twilight would stay away a whole weekend? Jennet Trevor, I'm ashamed of you! Of course she will be back!" Something twisted within him at his words, a cold feeling they just might not be true. If Jenny caught it she didn't let on.

"I think I'll cancel my doctor's appointment. Maybe she'll come while I'm gone."

"That's silly," Jeff scoffed, fear clutching his heart. He knew Jenny must not put off her appointment, or the surgery, no matter what. He had called the doctor himself, and speed was imperative. She could not wait.

"I'll take you myself. Mrs. Matthewson will be here. If Twilight comes she can give her a note from us. In the meantime I'm going to get you a decent breakfast. Just what the doctor ordered!"

If things hadn't been so tragic Jenny would have enjoyed the sight of Jeff stalking between refrigerator and stove, table and cupboards. He turned out a good breakfast, and at his insistence Jenny forced down as much as she could. His assumed gaiety and the lifting of the fog and rain to expose a crystal-clear day did a lot for her spirits, and by the time they had to leave she was feeling better. She had written Twilight a note, leaving it in Mrs. Matthewson's hands. By now Mrs. Matthewson realized there was more going on than met the eye, but she wisely refrained from questions. Jenny would tell her when the time came.

When Twilight slipped in and took her clothing, leaving Jeff's ring and no note, Mrs. Matthewson had just run across the street for a few moments. The little lady who lived there had received a call that her husband had been hurt at work and although assured it was only a slight accident, she became so upset she called on Mrs. Matthewson to help her get a taxi and put some things back in the purse she had dropped. The kindly landlady was unable to refuse, but before she went she opened the girls' apartment door and propped up Jenny's white envelope on the dresser. When Twilight came she had tossed her purse to the dresser in her haste to pack and get away. The note slipped and fell to the floor, unnoticed as the frantic girl stuffed things in suitcases and fled before anyone could come home. So when Jeff and Jenny got back, it was to find the ring box on the table, the closet half empty, and on the floor the letter that could have straightened everything out:

Dear Twilight,
 I am very sick. I have to go in for surgery on Monday. That is why Jeff was comforting me yesterday. I had just found out. Will be right back,
                    Your loving sister,
                    Jenny

If Jenny had been upset before, it was nothing compared to her face when she saw the bedroom. Wordlessly she turned to Jeff, holding out the ring box with the beautiful ring Twilight had loved so well.
 "She means it then." The words hung in the air. Without a sound, Jeff savagely shoved

the box in his pocket. Good thing he'd found out how childish Twilight could be, he told himself, even as a kind of sickness formed within. A low moan from Jenny recalled him to a need far greater than his own.

"We can still find her," he spoke as reasonably as he could. "Let me try some calling. Some of her friends will know where she is."

Cautiously, in even tones, he called all of her friends he could think of, asking simply if Twilight had arrived yet. Always the answer was the same: No, she hadn't planned on being with them at this time. With each call his fine face became more drawn, and Jenny's whiter and more still.

At last Jenny raised her head.

"It's no use. We've tried everyone."

"What about that aunt of yours? Lucy, isn't it? Suppose Twilight might have gone there?"

"Oh, no," Jenny responded. "I'm sure she wouldn't have even dreamed of leaving Seattle. Maybe she's in a hotel."

Again Jeff started calling, inquiring for a Miss Twilight Trevor at the hotels listed alphabetically, determinedly going down the list, one by one. No sir, sorry, no one by that name was registered. Ironically, the particular hotel Twilight had chosen had been so far out on the bus line it was listed in a suburbs directory rather than the city directory.

Saturday passed. Sunday came, dark and drear, unusual for the Puget Sound area in September. The hours dragged by. Jenny and Jeff had gone to Mr. and Mrs. Matthewson and told them the whole story. Because they were not so involved, it was easier for them to be objective.

"She's hurt, and disbelieving her own eyes, and scared," Mr. Matthewson pointed out wisely. "Give her some time to think. She'll come through. Let her alone."

"What else can we do?" Jeff replied bitterly. He went on to explain how they had to get in touch with her because of Jenny's surgery. But they had no practical help to offer.

"I still think we should contact your Aunt Lucy," Jeff said, but Jenny disagreed.

"She would only worry. She can't leave Stehekin right now, she's taken over substitute teaching for a while until there is a replacement. She would feel she'd have to come here and take care of me."

"No need for that," Mrs. Matthewson agreed warmly. "We'll just move you right in our extra downstairs bedroom when you get home. It's been a long time since I had a chick to fuss over. It will give me something to do!" Her words brought a laugh in spite of the tense situation, since Mrs. Matthewson was the busiest person they knew. Her garden, the talk of the neighborhood, churchwork, and sewing kept her on her toes. Yet she always found time for helping others. She would take good care of Jenny, whom she loved dearly.

Late Sunday evening Jeff took Jenny to the hospital where she had to sign papers and get checked in. After they had prepared her for the night he came back in for a moment.

"Jenny, this will probably be the hardest night you ever face. I asked them to give you a sleeping pill. Wait," he silenced her involuntary protest. "I know you don't like the stuff. But you must be relaxed tomorrow and worrying over your sister won't help. The best help you can be is to concentrate on getting well. I feel now like Mr. Matthewson said. When Twilight gets time to think she will know somehow that in spite of what she saw there has to be an explanation. Your job is to be well and happy so when she comes back she won't feel the terrible remorse that you went through this alone." Jeff realized that by an appeal for Twilight's sake Jenny could be reached. Her eyes brightened and she held out her thin hand.

"Thanks, Jeff." Her words were low, soft, but some of the strain had eased from her face.

"Time's up," a smiling white-capped nurse told him, coming to the bed with a capsule and glass of water. Jenny obediently took it, then smiled bravely as Jeff made a victory signal to her from the doorway.

"See you tomorrow."

The valiant look of her brought a fine mist to Jeff's eyes as he got in his car. What a girl! And her sister thought she was a traitor! Again hot anger at Twilight burned in him. Yet he remembered Mr. Matthewson's words ". . . hurt . . . disbelieving . . . scared." Shutting his eyes against the sudden pain, he could only lean his head against the car window. How could things have come to such a place? How could the most important thing in life be taken from him — and from Jenny?

But more important than either of them was the question, Where was Twilight? I must search for her, he thought. But I don't know where to start. She's too fine to harm herself, but where can she be? Starting the car and driving slowly home, he retraced the events of the past three days, trying to find another clue. She seemed to have vanished into thin air. Twilight was gone.

Chapter 5

Somewhere beyond the wooly gray curtain encasing her someone was calling.

"Jenny. Jenny, wake up."

Slowly the brown eyes opened, focused. An anxious-faced Jeff stood by the bedside next to the capable nurse holding Jenny's left wrist.

"She's fine," the nurse assured Jeff, smiling. She sensed more than usual interest for the young patient. The tall young man had spent the hours during the delicate operation on Jenny's heart, surgery to create a new channel for blood to course through, pacing the waiting room, waiting — waiting — waiting. Now she was glad to be able to tell him Jenny was going to be fine. She had come through the surgery with flying colors. Another week in the hospital followed by complete rest and "You'll be better than new," the nurse said with a laugh. Her voice sobered, and she gave Jeff a warning glance. "The only thing is, Jenny must be very quiet. No activity for a while. She must mend." She turned to the girl lying so still.

"You have a sister to take care of you when we let you go home, don't you?"

Unexpected tears filled the young girl's eyes as she falteringly tried to reply.

"I — I won't be staying with my sister."

Jeff hurriedly cut in, "Her sister is away just now, but there's a wonderful lady —" He went on to describe Mrs. Matthewson. The nurse listened intently, making notes on her chart, sensing something happening in regard to the sister yet unwilling to press the point.

"She sounds like 'just what the doctor ordered,' " the nurse reassured Jenny, patting the white hand. "There's no one better to have around when you're recuperating than someone cheerful and kindly." She turned to Jeff.

"Time's up. She's had enough company for a while. Looks like you could use a cup of coffee. The cafeteria makes a good hot brew. Why don't you let this little gal get some rest? You can come back later today."

Jeff reluctantly agreed. He could see the well-meaning nurse's question about Twilight had thrown Jenny off her stride. He hated to leave, but the nurse was insistent, and she was right. Jenny had to rest.

When they had gone, Jenny obediently closed her eyes but sleep had fled. She felt alert. There was no pain, just a tightness in her chest where she was bandaged. How good it was she had come through so well!

I must look on the bright side, she told herself. What if I hadn't made it? She shivered. The doctor had told her how serious the surgery was the day he insisted on going ahead. She remembered the way he patted her hand as he said, "Jenny, I'm afraid you won't be entering nurse's training this fall."

Quick fear had leaped to her eyes. Her dream was to be a nurse. What had he found in her pre-nursing physical?

"You must have had something wrong with your heart for a long time that just didn't show up," he told her. Then came question after question. Had she felt overly tired lately? Was she losing weight? Did she ever have what she might have felt were muscle pains? Jenny had to answer yes to his queries. Then came the final question.

"Have you told your sister you haven't been feeling well?"

"Well, no," Jenny had admitted. "She's been so busy looking forward to the wedding, finishing a quick couple of classes at the U. and so forth we haven't had as much time together lately. I didn't dream anything could really be wrong with me." Her voice trembled. Ever since she could remember she had only wanted to do one thing — become a

58

nurse. Now her family doctor was telling her kindly but firmly it was out of the question. Even if her heart wasn't demanding immediate attention she was in no physical condition to take on a strenuous nursing schedule.

Sensing the question she was afraid to voice the good old doctor again patted her hand.

"In a year, Jenny. If your surgery goes well, and there is every reason to hope it will, you will be built up until your dream can be realized, and when it does, I'll do everything in my power to see that you get a scholarship just as you were this time."

Bitter tears of disappointment fell down Jenny's face.

"How can I tell Twilight?" she choked. "It was all settled. She and Jeff are getting married and I was going to live with them and get in my training. Now everything's spoiled."

The doctor's crisp words dried her tears.

"It would be a lot more spoiled if this hadn't been discovered. You could have collapsed in class or on a ward. Then it would have been too late to correct. You're really lucky, Jenny, that such a rigorous physical is required for pre-nursing."

In spite of his reassurance when Jenny had reached the apartment she was still almost numb with shock. I must tell Twilight, she thought. But maybe I should tell Jeff first. It might be easier if he were here. Twilight would be sick at the thought of the surgery and postponement of the dream she shared completely with her younger sister. After dialing Jeff, she paced the floor until he came. When he stepped into the room, she flew to him as to a rock of strength.

Now she shut her mind on the rest of the scene. It was too hard to relive Twilight's entrance. I must get well, she told herself fiercely. As soon as they let me I'm going to find Twilight if I have to comb everyplace in the country. She can't just disappear. She's too unusual looking. A slight grin replaced some of the tension in her face. With Twilight's unusual name and coloring she was outstanding in any crowd. Fortunately for Jenny's peace of mind she never even thought Twilight might be using another name. If she had, it would have been a much longer time before she could wearily sink back to the healing powers of deep sleep and let go all the troubles in her young life.

Perhaps it was her great determination, but just a week later she was released to Mrs. Matthewson's tender care. It was quite an event. The Matthewsons had hastily re-arranged their spare bedroom, freshening it with soft new curtains framing the window that looked out over the waters of Lake Washington. It would be a perfect place to recuperate. Autumn was in full swing. The trees in the yard had finished their dressing up for the year and were now beginning to discard a few leaves, preparatory to changing color. It was a large, sunny room, old-fashioned yet homey. Big enough for the double bed, dresser, desk, and even a rocker, it seemed a haven to Jenny as she was carried in by Jeff. She hadn't realized how much the short trip from the hospital would tax her frail strength. It was good to be tucked in by Mrs. Matthewson. Across the rocker lay the yellow quilted robe Jeff and bought and on the floor beneath were the matching slippers from the Matthewsons. They had gone together to find what Jenny would like.

Again quick tears filled her eyes at their goodness, but a shadow crept into them, a wistfulness. If only they could find Twilight! In the week and a half Jenny had been hospitalized there had been no trace. Jeff had again approached every friend he could name, this time telling them she had seemingly disappeared. How could she vanish? He checked with her college professors. No, Miss Trevor had not been in class since Friday — it was always the same. No one knew where Twilight was.

Jeff wanted to contact Aunt Lucy at

Stehekin but once more Jenny shook her head.

"Wait until I'm better," she begged. "It would only worry her." Her face brightened.

"Jeff, maybe in a few weeks when I'm better I can go see her. I know she'd love to have me."

Jeff wasn't too sure about that. "I don't think there's a doctor up there, Jenny. You have to be where you can get your regular checkups."

The light in her face died. "I guess you're right. Well, maybe next spring . . ." Her voice trailed off, losing interest.

Jeff's steady gray eyes met Mrs. Matthewson's concerned look across the bed.

"Of course, honey," she told Jenny. "It's getting on toward winter, and they have some real dillies up there! You don't want to get up there in all the ice and snow. Besides, now that I've got a girl of my own again, you needn't think I'm going to let her go that fast!" She was rewarded with the faint smile that had become so much a part of Jenny the last few days.

"Thank you, Mrs. Matthewson," she said quietly. "I can't think of anyone who would be so good to me." There was a gentle dignity about her that forestalled further comment and with a quick wave Mrs. Matthewson and

Jeff slipped away, leaving her to her own thoughts.

In the days and weeks that followed Jenny was an ideal patient. She obediently ate what was brought to her, expressing appreciation for the flowers or clever cards that appeared on her tray. She slept, restlessly, and when she grew stronger took walks with Jeff and Mr. Matthewson. Gradually her face began to fill out, her cheeks began to reflect the rosiness of the winter sunsets. She was quieter than before, but that was natural. A shadow still hung in her eyes, clouding the clear brown, giving her an air of sadness even when she forgot Twilight for a moment and laughed heartily. She had made friends immediately with one of the neighbor's cats, and when kittens were produced Mr. Matthewson brought her a tiny bundle of fur. Various shades of gray combined with a white streak between the ears gave the kitten a diabolical look and as Smokey grew, it seemed to fit. He was into everything, but the Matthewsons were willing to put up with his antics just to hear Jenny laugh.

She didn't mention Twilight so much now. Jeff had accepted a temporary assignment in the Mount Baker National Forest and was away during the week. On weekends he was her faithful devoted brother, planning little outings for her, a drive to the mountains, a stroll in one of the many Seattle parks, or along the waterfront, sometimes just a ferry-boat ride to Vashon or one of the other islands.

I'm marking time, Jenny told herself one crisp afternoon in January. I'm just almost holding my breath waiting for spring. When spring comes I'm going to Aunt Lucy and tell her the whole thing. She has a lot of friends with influence. Maybe she can help me. Maybe I should have told her sooner. But I couldn't, she salved her conscience. She would have dropped everything and come. I don't think I could have stood it to see her every day, wondering, worrying about Twilight. It's been bad enough for me. I couldn't give her that worry. It never once crossed her mind that Twilight too might have felt like fleeing to Aunt Lucy. She had decided, and Jeff and the Matthewsons agreed with her, that Twilight must have taken a job with a small school somewhere and was keeping out of sight that way.

January passed, then February. In early March the flowers began to spring into being, coloring the sidewalk edges, adding bright-ness to the streets. Children discarded winter clothing, glad to be free of encumbering jackets and boots. The sound was clear and blue, white sailboats dotted both it and Lake Washington. Woodland Park with its zoo again welcomed crowds of visitors. The Space Needle superciliously observed the new life of those on spring shopping sprees downtown. Basketball gave way to baseball, skiing in the mountains to walking in the parks. All this time Jenny grew in strength. Her doctor was amazed. He knew something was troubling her mentally, yet her physical condition was better than it had been before surgery.

"You will be able to go into training next fall if you still want to," he told the glowing girl on her spring visit to him. "You check out just fine."

Suddenly he was enveloped by two arms in a bear hug and a pair of starry eyes shining at him.

"You really mean it?" Jenny breathed, happiness erasing the sadness of the past winter months.

"I certainly do," he replied gruffly to cover his own emotion.

Wordlessly she took his hand, then walked out of the office with head high. She was well! She could make her plans! Even Twilight's absence could not touch that moment of pure joy. With such a blue and gold day heralding the approach of spring there was no room for depression. The fears of the winter when she had thought maybe she would never find Twilight vanished as fog before a hot sun over the sound. Hope replaced it. She would find Twilight. She would show Twilight how well she was.

Somehow the pavement didn't even feel hard beneath her feet. She skipped, then ran, then just stopped and looked around her. A policeman touched his cap respectfully. "Good morning, miss."

"Good morning, and isn't it a wonderful one!" she replied, with such enthusiasm that her sparkling face stayed with him the rest of the day and helped lighten his duties.

"Mrs. Matthewson!" Jenny burst into the kitchen where her good friend was setting homemade bread. The lady always told everyone that "store-boughten bread" wasn't fit to eat. She preferred her own — and so did everyone who came to her home! Whole wheat, half and half, or crusty white. Each more delicious than the other. Now she lifted her head, instantly alert to the happiness in her young charge's voice.

Like the doctor, she was almost smothered in a bear hug.

"Land sakes, child, you'll get flour all over you!" The good woman beamed.

"I don't care." Jenny pirouetted across the

kitchen floor. "I'm well! The doctor said so!"

Gone was all trace of bewilderment from Mrs. Matthewson. Now it was her turn to scoop Jenny into her welcoming arms.

"Praise the Lord!"

Jenny laughed. "Yes, you're right! All winter I've really wondered if they were being truthful with me. How could I have heart surgery and still be strong? But now —" Her eyes took on a dreamy look.

"Now it's time for spring."

Mrs. Matthewson's words claimed Jenny's full attention.

"Yes. Winter is past. It's time for spring."

Glancing keenly at the happy girl, Mrs. Matthewson slowly took a folded newspaper off the top of the refrigerator, pointing to a marked item.

"It's a wonder I saw it," she commented. Curious, Jenny took the paper, reading the tiny article buried between world and local items. In a few words it told a more or less interested reading audience that as of February 16 Sunday mail boat service was resumed to Stehekin. It went on to mention some of the items available at Stehekin, such as interdenominational church services for those who cared to attend, and commenting that for those interested in making it a permanent place to live there was a one-room school presided over by a "Miss Angel," who was doing a lot for the students.

"Then she isn't substituting any more!" Jenny beamed. "Now I can feel even freer about going to see Aunt Lucy." She bounded out of the kitchen, sticking her head back in long enough to add, "I'm writing to her immediately. If she answers right back I'll plan to go as soon as I can. Won't it be fun if I'm there in time for Easter? It said they meet in an old Golden West Lodge. Aunt Lucy always liked to go to church. Sounds really good."

Mrs. Matthewson smiled at the eager girl.

"Go get your letter written. Then I need you to go to the store for me. I'm almost out of milk and can't make the chowder I want to go with this fresh bread."

A sigh escaped her lips as Jenny danced away. She had grown to love the beautiful young girl even more during the time she had lived with them. The struggle she had faced, the way she had kept on keeping on, all were part of her dearness.

The flour-covered hands stilled. The shapeless mass of dough was still. A tear fell to the rolling pin laid out for cookies when the bread was finished, as a quick prayer rose to the good woman's lips.

"Please, let her find Twilight."

Chapter 6

A small smile of satisfaction touched Twilight's lips as she surveyed the ten busy students, heads bent, absorbed in their studies. A little sigh of relief escaped her and the tenseness in her shoulder blades relaxed. It was almost time to go home, the end of her first day as substitute teacher, as Miss Angel.

Aunt Lucy was right, she thought. When I wrote Miss Angelica on the board Tommy's hand shot up.

"It's too hard for the little ones to say, teacher. Can't we just call you Miss Angel?"

"That will be fine," she had responded.

Her eyes traveled from head to head, remembering the way she had diligently memorized the names of each pupil and the witty but accurate descriptions Aunt Lucy had given until this morning she had stood with heart pounding, greeting each by name as they entered. The little ones had come in wide-eyed, unsure of what to expect. The middle graders giggled, and the eighth graders wore an air of sophistication. After all, wasn't this their last year in the one-room school? Next year, if they chose to get further education, they would have to go to Chelan or Manson.

Twilight's gaze dropped to the neat chart before her.

Class list

Grade	Name/Parents' Name	Description
1	Honey Jacobsen (Jingles)	Small, blonde, shy.
1	Tara Wilson (Frank)	Plain until shown something with beauty, then radiates.
3	Pixie Jones (Gordon)	Her name really is Pixie! It fits. She's a laughing dark elfin child.
4	Rusty Jones (Gordon)	Also fits, reddish hair, freckles, good-natured.
5	Tommy Jacobsen (Jingles)	Natural protector because of bear incident.

6	Pam Richards (Clint)	Dark, beautiful, sullen? Watch for mischief beneath apparently innocent manner.
6	Penny Richards	Pam's twin, a follower to Pam's lead.
8	Mike Cummings (Miles)	Another redhead, almost as tall as Twilight. Best student if can spark interest.
8	Columbine Jones (Gordon)	Fair, pretty, enjoys attention of both boys in her grade.
8	Frank Wilson, Jr. (Frank)	Steady, depend-able.

Twilight added notations to the bottom of Aunt Lucy's carefully prepared list.

Parents: Jingles, I know. *Frank Wilson,* have met — works for Jingles, Aunt Lucy's neighbor. *Gordon Jones,* on leave from his newspaper for a year, working on a special writing project. *Clint Richards,* National Park

Service. (Could this account for the bit of uppishness in Pam and Penny?) *Miles Cummings,* widower, National Park Service, early to mid-thirties.

Dropping her list, Twilight caught Tommy's eye on her, his forefinger determinedly pointing to the clock. With an answering smile she announce, "Class dismissed."

Her students reacted typically, the boys out the door with a rush, the little girls hesitating near teacher's desk, Columbine between Frank, Jr., and Mike as she went out with a smile over her shoulder for Twilight.

When they had all gone, the stiffening seemed to leave her knees, and she dropped to a chair behind her desk and surveyed the room. Spotlessly clean, a small bouquet of wildflowers was wilting in a glass jar. I must remember to ask Aunt Lucy for a vase, she thought. Honey's earnest face flashed through Twilight's memory as she brought in the handful of "posies," as she called them. Then one by one the faces of her other pupils flashed before her. The expressions of boredom giving way to genuine interest as they spent some time in just "getting acquainted." The loud hooray followed by shamed silence to see what her reaction would be when she announced the first day would be dismissed a little early. The answering grins when she too smiled.

There had been no discipline problems. For one thing, they had been too busy! From roll call to dismissal Twilight had kept them hopping. Even the dinner break, as it was called, was full of some new organized games she had learned at the U. Little had she dreamed that she would first teach them in a log-cabin school in a remote wilderness! But how they were appreciated! She made sure the smaller ones were included as well as the older pupils.

There had only been one bad moment. When Twilight announced they would take out their Social Studies books, the three eighth graders groaned.

"What's the use of studying all that?" Mike Cummings wanted to know. "I can see why we need arithmetic, reading, all that stuff. But what good is geography and history?"

At a loss for a moment, Twilight's natural feelings took over. She had determined never to close the door to questioning. This was her first opportunity.

"Let's talk about it," she told them quietly. Columbine and Frank, Jr., had nodded agreement to Mike's comment. Thinking fast, Twilight spoke.

"I've changed my mind. Put your books

back." She noted Mike's and Frank, Jr.'s exchange of glances but chose to ignore it.

"I'm going to give you a different type of Social Studies lesson. For tomorrow I want each of you to bring me a short essay about the area you live in. We'll start our study of Social Studies right here in Stehekin." Silence greeted her statement, then as usual, Mike took the lead.

"An essay? You mean like in English? What's supposed to be in it, teacher?"

Twilight smiled at him. "Anything about this country you think I might be interested in learning!" Frank, Jr., laughed right out, quickly smothering the noise in his sleeve as the two sixth-grade twins looked up inquiringly.

"Go on with your work," Twilight told them.

Columbine's pretty brow was wrinkled. "You mean stuff like about the lake and the country?"

"That's right, Columbine." Twilight moved her chair nearer to the three, her earnestness reaching them.

"I am a total stranger to your country. I don't know how long I'll be here, but I would like to learn all there is to know about your home. Don't try to be too formal, just write things you know, or that your folks can tell you. Then we can compare some of it with other places and countries and see how it is the same, and what the differences are."

Interest sparkled in Mike's eyes but he only grunted, "Awright." Yet as she sent them back to their places Twilight noticed all three eagerly reaching for paper. Now and then one of them would cast a speculating gaze at her while she worked with the little ones.

With a start Twilight saw Tommy waiting for her in the doorway.

"Time to go, Miss Angel."

Hurriedly she gathered up her "dinner bucket," lessons, and satchel. Tommy had another walk home after seeing her safely back to Aunt Lucy's. On the way home she pelted him with questions. Some of the things she had taken for granted were completely wrong. When she innocently asked where the horses were tied when the children brought them in bad weather Tommy vainly tried to repress a grin but burst out laughing

"We don't ride horses. Our folks bring us in pickups or snow cats."

Twilight's eyes opened wide. Snow cats! No horses? Then she laughed at herself, enjoying the joke as hugely as Tommy.

"Don't give me away to the others," she told him. "I'm just a greenhorn."

Hero worship filled the boy's eyes. "You

can ask me anything you want, Miss Angel," he answered with dignity. "I won't pass it on."

Aunt Lucy chuckled over Twilight's day.

"Glad to see you using your initiative! Social Studies is one of the hardest classes to get up a real interest in here. Somehow when these youngsters are away from all the rush and hustle, reading about wars and customs in other lands isn't important to them. They are involved with real living, facing daily problems of survival, especially in winter. Best thing you can ever do is take exactly the approach you did. Relate it to them, to now."

"I can hardly wait to read their essays," Twilight confessed. She sat silently for a few moments, then her voice shook a bit.

"Do you know, Aunt Lucy, you were right — I never once thought of Jeff or Jenny today."

Aunt Lucy wisely refrained from commenting, only patted her hand and smiled. She had known Twilight would be too busy to even think, let alone brood, with ten active students in her charge!

The next day found all of the students in their places after a crisp morning walk for most, although Mike Cummings drove every day from the National Park Service Headquarters, bringing the Richards twins with him. He had just turned sixteen and was tremendously proud of his license. He was also extremely careful with his driving. Evidently his father had managed to instill in him not only the joy but the responsibility involved.

When Social Studies period came Columbine begged for a little more time to finish her essay. Mike and Frank, Jr., backed her up.

"There's so much to say it's hard to know where to start," they pleaded. Twilight realized there is a time to be firm and a time to bend. This was a time to be pliant to their needs. Genuine interest was accompanying this assignment.

"You may take the rest of today's class," she compromised. "But do the best you can. I want to take those essays home with me this afternoon." Despite their looks of dismay she held firm to that point.

"There will be more opportunity. After we've discussed some of what you tell me, more things will come to mind."

There wasn't a sound out of her eighth graders for the rest of the day, and when she called dismissal each reacted typically. Mike signed his paper with a flourish, Columbine lingered to daintily arrange her pages, and Frank, Jr., hastily erased a misspelled word and corrected it.

"Will you read them tonight?" Mike wanted to know.

"Yes," Twilight promised. "We can discuss them in class tomorrow."

As good as her word, that evening after supper and dishes were done Twilight settled down before the fire with her papers. Aunt Lucy was lost in a good book she had dug out of some old boxes while looking for material for Twilight's classes, but curiosity kept her from total involvement with the imaginary heroes and heroines. Gradually even the most thrilling pages lost their flavor and at last she shut the covers with a bang.

"What did you find that was interesting in your essays?" she asked. Twilight raised her glowing face.

"Oh, Aunt Lucy, you can't imagine what a good job they did! Let me read you some excerpts." She shuffled the pages in her hands.

"Lake Chelan . . . meaning deep water . . . forty-eight streams and one river flow to lake . . . twenty-seven glaciers . . . fifty point two miles long . . . second deepest fresh water lake in the United States —" She paused, then asked, "What is the first?"

"Crater Lake."

"Good! I'll tell them tomorrow." She went back to her papers.

"It says here it is one thousand five hundred and eighty-six feet deep with a seventy-five mile shoreline. Why, when you double that for the other side then it's a hundred and fifty miles!" Again she turned a page.

"Mike writes the lake's average temperature is below thirty-four degrees, that the upper twenty-one feet is man-made, a dam going in in nineteen twenty-seven. I don't know how accurate he is, but he must really have done some asking questions last night!" She laid his aside.

"Columbine mentions more about the place itself than the lake. She goes into the kind of people who live here — government employees, concession personnel, retirees, shop owners. She says fifty to seventy yearround folks are here. She notes there is a retired doctor here now, not practicing but who in case of emergency could help out." She read on silently for a moment then exclaimed,

"She says Stehekin Valley is fifty-five miles long, that it ranges from over five thousand four hundred feet wide down here to very narrow at Cascade Pass."

Again Twilight concentrated on the essays. Finishing Columbine's, she picked up Frank, Jr.'s.

"Frank must be interested in transportation. He mentions that while you have radio phone out, there is no phone in, that access is by water, air, or trail. Air?"

"Yes," Aunt Lucy replied. "We have a small airport but it is adequate for our needs." Twilight could tell by her expression that Aunt Lucy was enjoying the essays hugely.

She read on.

"Eighteen feet of snow in the valley Surely Frank, Jr., must be joking!"

"Not necessarily. We get a lot. I wouldn't confirm quite that much but neither would I say he is wrong."

"But how do you manage?" Twilight gasped. Something in her aunt's calm reply rang a tiny bell in Twilight's consciousness, jelling some of her growing convictions about this amazing place and the people in it.

"We help one another."

Long after Twilight was in bed that night the four little words rang through her brain.

"We help one another." What a world of meaning in the simple statement! No wonder the people she met were so warm and openhearted. Survival depended on them working together. There was no time for bitterness or feuds. Aunt Lucy had said the area was "gossipy but neighborly." Twilight laughed to herself. She could imagine that! There didn't appear to be a whole lot of entertainment but then, she thought, are people really better off with it? Here the people work hard and enjoy one another. Back in Seattle we rush around like a swarm of bees, never really taking the time to know any but the very few we are in daily contact with, never knowing even our next-door neighbors.

That is, most of us, she amended, remembering the Matthewsons. With a sudden clarity of vision Twilight thought, They are like the people here. Concerned. Caring. I wonder — will I be like that?

Her last waking thought was of the next day at school and what it would bring. What can I give the community? Suddenly a thought flashed through her mind. I was good in college drama — I wonder if my students would like to do a play, maybe for Thanksgiving? Or Christmas? I'll ask Aunt Lucy tomorrow.

She was too sleepy to pursue the thought further. For a quick moment Jeff's face seemed to float above her, but for the first time there was no pain in her heart. She felt removed from Jeff and Jenny — they had to do with another world, seemingly a lifetime ago. The duties of her teaching, combined with a half-mile walk each morning and evening, were doing their work well. She was too sleepy by the end of the day to worry over the past, too busy during the day.

She knew, Twilight thought, nearly asleep, or was she dreaming? Aunt Lucy knew. A gentle sigh and she was asleep. Her dreams were untroubled with memories. The knowledge of her importance to her ten students had done what no amount of rationalizing could have accomplished — started to give her peace.

Chapter 7

Twilight pulled her heavy coat closer against the chill air. In the short weeks since she had come to Stehekin fall had given way to winter. She was still walking to school each morning but it wouldn't last long — the chill, gray sky evidenced that. Lucky she had heeded Aunt Lucy's advice and learned to drive the jeep. Next week was Thanksgiving week and more than likely would bring snow. She was secretly looking forward to it. Snow in Seattle was just an inconvenience, but up here where people were prepared for it, she could hardly wait.

Thanksgiving! In spite of her rapidly dimming pain over Jeff and Jenny, Twilight's heart was full. When had she been busier, or more needed? She laughed outright at the enthusiasm her idea of a play had generated. Not only the students but the entire community was looking forward to Wednesday evening before school was out for the long weekend! With Aunt Lucy's help, Twilight had decided not to use a formal play.

"Store-boughten plays are all right elsewhere," Aunt Lucy advised. She laughed at Twilight's involuntary quirk of her eyebrows at the unfamiliar colloquialism.

"Yes, 'store-boughten.' Can you think of a better word?"

Twilight had to admit she couldn't. More and more she was learning to appreciate the homely expressions and ways of life she found.

"We can turn out a homemade play that everyone will like," had been Aunt Lucy's decree, so one weekend with wind howling outside and a cozy fire inside they had written their program.

Twilight thought of it now. Appropriately named *The First Thanksgiving*, she and Aunt Lucy had woven in the story not only all the drama of the hardship and thankfulness the Pilgrims had known but also the personality of the students portraying each character. Pixie and the Richards twins, Pam and Penny, were beautiful as Indian maidens. Rusty Jones with his freckles and natural curiosity fit the outgoing friendly boy of the story. Frank Wilson made an excellent father, Columbine was wife and mother, while Mike stole the show as Squanto. His strutting across the front of the schoolroom was not only accurate but delightful. He loved the proud character he had been given.

Tommy was the settler boy who looked forward to Thanksgiving for one thing — to eat! He was always hungry, never full. His little sister Honey and Tara Wilson were charming in their sober Pilgrim garb. The entire group had worked hard, and now on the Friday before Thanksgiving Twilight unlocked the school door with anticipation. Today they would work on a few simple stage settings. Colored pictures for the background made by the younger children. A worn old sheet for a curtain, decorated with textile paint in the middle graders' interpretation of what were supposed to be Indian designs. But the pièce de résistance was the turkey. It had posed a problem. They must have an authentic-looking turkey for the feast in the play, but how? Obviously they couldn't haul a cooked turkey to school!

Frank had solved the problem by creating one. Using chicken wire and bending it into the proper shape, he covered it expertly with brown wrapping paper, completed it with two drumsticks waving wildly in the air, and settled it on a life-size platter garnished with parsley, which his mother grew in her tiny garden spot. It was a masterpiece! You could almost smell it from a distance, Twilight thought, laughing at her childish eagerness.

It was a happy day and they were all so absorbed in their work no one noticed the sharp drop in temperature until midafternoon when Honey looked out the window.

"It's snowing!" she announced gleefully, disrupting the little group at their work. Twilight rushed to the window along with her pupils. Indeed it was snowing, and hard! Casting an anxious glance at the clock, she saw it was still an hour until dismissal time. Tommy intercepted her look.

"Don't worry, Miss Angel. There'll be plenty of rides home." True to his words, when school was over a strange assortment of vehicles stood at the door. Mike, of course, had his father's pickup, well equipped for winter. He took the Richards girls, then crowded in Pixie, Rusty, and Columbine, promising to drop them at home. Jingles was there for Tommy and Honey, good-naturedly ordering them into the rear of the jeep so Miss Angel could sit by him. But Frank Wilson surpassed them all. He had an old wagonbed mounted on what looked to be homemade skis. Fastened with a trailer hitch to his ancient pickup, it was filled with hay. A string of bells rang merrily through the rapidly increasing snow.

Twilight caught her breath involuntarily, her great purple eyes aglow. "Oh!" It was all she could say.

"Wait until there's a little more snow," Frank, Jr., promised. True to his word, the next evening about seven o'clock the clash of bells enticed Twilight to the front porch of Aunt Lucy's cabin. There in full regalia, bundled to the ears, were most of her pupils from the valley, along with a few grownups.

"Get your duds on," Frank called, and his little birdlike wife seconded,

"We're going to the Joneses.' "

If I live to be a hundred I will never forget this, Twilight thought. It was an evening to be remembered, also repeated, throughout the long Stehekin winter, yet the first time was so special because of its very newness.

It had snowed all night Friday and until about four o'clock on Saturday afternoon, then gradually dwindled until a lopsided moon had come out. The temperature had dropped again, leaving the snow packed and beautiful. Great billows of it hung on the evergreen trees. Gobs and heaps and tons of it seemed piled along the valley floor where they slowly traveled. In the distance dark water ran lazily between iced banks — soon it would be frozen. Even the air seemed to sparkle with cleanliness and beauty. It hurt to breathe deeply and Twilight wrapped the thin silk scarf across her face loosely as Aunt Lucy had told her. There was something about the night that spelled promise, something primitive, mysterious.

They don't sense it, Twilight thought, looking at her pupils. They are so used to it they don't even see. A pang of disappointment shot through her. How could anyone become immune to such beauty? Her eyes rested on little Tara Wilson and her heart leaped. The plain face was alight. She wasn't singing with the rest, just sitting here looking. Twilight moved a little closer and put her arm around the little girl. Although not a word passed between them, a bond was formed. Tara could feel Twilight's own response to the magnificent night.

It seemed but moments until they were stamping their boots and shedding heavy garments at the Joneses'. More people were there, many of them she hadn't met, Twilight realized. The Jones family lived in an old-fashioned house, two story, lots of room. As was the case in so many Stehekin homes, the fireplace was the center of attraction. Right now its glory was dimmed a bit by the enticing aroma of hot oyster stew from the kitchen, soon borne in by willing hands, ladled into heavy bowls, and consumed by the hungry sleigh-riders. Twilight was ashamed of the way she ate but Aunt Lucy, who had come along with them, cast and all, told her,

"Eat hearty, dear. It insulates you against the cold."

When the last drop was gone, and the last crumb of the delicious lemon pound cake, they sang around the fireplace until they were all hoarse.

Twilight had been content to just be one of the group, but when she caught the beautiful harmony of the voices she cried out, "You should have a community choir!" Faces stared at her blankly and she drew back, wishing she hadn't spoken so freely, but after a moment Jingles nodded assent.

"Don't see why not! Can't do too much in winter anyway. You'll direct us, Miss Angel?"

Other voices took up the question. "Miss Angel? Will you?" Laughing, she made a futile motion of protest, then nodded.

"I don't know much about music for adults but we could have some fun this winter." Before she knew it she had agreed for them to meet in the schoolhouse one evening a week starting the week after Thanksgiving. They would stick to simple melodies and Christmas songs and if things went well —

"We can have our own Christmas concert," Miles Cummings put in.

Twilight looked at him wonderingly. She had been drawn to the apparently lonely man, Mike's father. He looked older than mid-thirty, and she remembered the story of his wife's death not too long before. Miles was with the National Park Service and when they found out his wife was afflicted with incurable cancer she had chosen to stay on in Stehekin. Six weeks after discovery she was gone, leaving Miles to make a home for his boy. Twilight could see in young Mike the promise of a great man. He idolized his father, and now Twilight was happy to see the man was evidently worthy of his son's regard.

He reminds me of Jeff, she thought suddenly. Calm, unstampedable. For a moment the old pain twisted her heart, bringing a quick rush of tears to her eyes, but she blinked them back furiously. I can't cry here, she scolded herself. What's wrong with me! To escape further emotion she caught up the Jones baby, a wee mite of six months, and held it close. He was a precious little boy, and Twilight had noticed the way Columbine and even young Pixie hung over his crib. She never knew Aunt Lucy's wise old eyes had caught the sudden influx of tears.

"All aboard!" Frank Wilson was calling from the door. There was a rush to get back into winter clothing and climb into the sleigh. Those who couldn't crowd into it rode in the back of Miles's pickup, also now warmly lined with hay for the event.

If the ride over had been beautiful, the ride home was glorious. Even colder, there was a snap in the night defying description. Long icicles hung from some of the branches. The moon and stars seemed close enough to reach up and touch. There was scarcely need for the vehicles' headlights it was so light. They had told Twilight that with a little more snow it would be snow cat time. She looked forward to it. She also looked forward to the "singing school," as it had been called.

Miles Cummings had drawn Twilight to one side.

"My wife had a lot of music, Christmas, holiday, all kinds. Shall I bring it?"

"That would be wonderful." She smiled at the tall man. "I must confess I was wondering how to get any by next week."

He laughed at her concern. "Everyone who comes will bring their hymn books — say, speaking of hymn books, I bet we can use them from the church services."

Twilight brightened. "I never thought of that!"

Now she remembered his quiet look of pleasure at her enthusiasm. Maybe I can help, she determined. He seems so lonely. It can't do any harm to get him involved in things, even more for Mike's sake than his own. Her chin raised a trifle in the endearing way she had when deciding a course of action. Again Aunt Lucy's keen eyes noted. Not much went past that good lady, although she was careful not to comment unless asked.

When they arrived home it was too late to talk, but the next afternoon while watching the blue and gold and crystal-clear day out the window, Twilight asked, "Aunt Lucy, do you think people would like it if we turned our Thanksgiving program into a little more of a social?"

Without waiting for a reply she rushed on. "I thought maybe after the children's play we could ask some of the adults to tell some Thanksgiving experience they remembered, or . . ." Her voice trailed off, but Aunt Lucy enthusiastically seconded the motion.

"That would be a great idea! A lot of folks don't get as much time just to chat as they should." She fell silent for a moment.

"Twilight, let's make it real fun time! I can get word to the different families and ask the mothers to bring cookies, or cake, or something. Most of us spend Thanksgiving apart, but the night before would be a good time for a party."

"Aunt Lucy, you're a dear!" Twilight impulsively hugged her aunt. "I can hardly wait!"

Neither, it seemed, could the pupils in Miss

Angel's school. All day Monday and Tuesday they were in a dither. Mysterious hints of what "Mama is making" reached Twilight's ears from her small pupils. The whole valley was anticipating the children's play.

At last Twilight announced Tuesday afternoon, "Tomorrow we will dismiss at noon. This will give us time to get ready for the evening. Remember the program starts at seven sharp, so you all need to be here not later than a quarter of seven."

She waved farewell from the doorway as they joyfully trooped away. Snow cats were among the vehicles being used now. True to Jingles's predictions, more snow had fallen and the valley was blanketed.

Twilight could never have told you after it was all over who had been more excited that Wednesday evening, she, her students, or the onlookers. *The First Thanksgiving* was a smash hit, so much so that before the applause had subsided, everyone was begging Miss Angel to write a Christmas play! Somewhere along the line she had ceased asking when they would find a replacement teacher. Her life had become so bound up with her work that she secretly longed to finish the school year.

For now it was enough to watch the charm and grace of her little ones, the Indians who tended to giggle, only adding to the holiday spirit of that first feast, and the lofty Squanto who strode across the stage as though he owned it! Pride stood in her eyes, reflected in the eyes of the parents and neighbors who had come. The little schoolhouse was crammed with people.

When the play was over Twilight stood and said simply, "Now it's your turn. Would some of you tell something you remember about Thanksgiving, or about a thankful time?"

Incorrigible Aunt Lucy started the ball rolling.

"Mine isn't the kind of Thanksgiving time you probably mean —" she hesitated, unwilling to say "Miss Angel" and biting back the word Twilight. Covering up her momentary lapse, she continued.

"Young Frank Wilson will remember this quite well, though." A general laugh followed as she related an incident from a few years back.

She had been teaching about the early days in America, especially on the Western frontier. It was a beautiful Indian summer day, so warm the windows were open to let in the remaining fall breezes. Under the window young Frank was reading aloud from his history book.

" '... and there was always the fear of being scalped. No one knew when the settlers might be attacked. . . .' " At that precise moment his father, who had come for the boy a little early, passed by the open window. He had a sense of humor and decided to play a trick on his son. He didn't hear the content of what was being read, all he saw was the bent head of his boy. A big hand crept through the open window, hesitated for a moment, then firmly grasped a thatch of young Frank's hair, giving it a playful tug.

Terror filled the boy's eyes and he rose right up out of the seat, face white as a sheet, shouting, "I'm scalped!"

Twilight and the others laughed till they cried, visualizing the scene. Aunt Lucy wiped her eyes and confessed, "There was no more school that day!"

Frank, Jr., looked sheepish, and his dad literally howled. He had almost forgotten that long-ago day.

One by one stories were told until at last Twilight asked, "Jingles, do you have a Thanksgiving story?"

The kindly man smiled at her, one hand buried in Honey's curls, the other on Tommy's shoulder.

"Yes, I do," he stated quietly. "Almost everyone here has heard it except you, but it is worth thinking about again." After a moment he began to speak.

"We all know this isn't the easiest country in the world to live in, yet we love it, that's why we stay. But sometimes its ways are hard, almost too hard." He cleared his throat of mistiness and went on, eyes searching out the different students, soft with remembrance.

"It wasn't that long ago we almost lost our most precious commodity — our children." His hand tightened.

"We all remember the blizzard, and what nearly happened." For a moment fear seemed to touch the room, then relaxation set in as Jingles told the story. An unexpected blizzard. A teacher new to the country and its perils. Children sent home when they should have been kept at the schoolhouse. Hours of tense waiting.

Twilight had heard the story over and over, sometimes in books, a few times on television. But never had she lived the despair and hope-lessness as she did now. These children she loved had been involved. They were the ones who had struggled in the drifts until after anx-ious hours one by one they were found and restored to warmth and security.

"We have much to be thankful for," Jingles concluded, his honest face wet with unashamed tears, reflected in the eyes and hearts of many.

"Whoa, now, didn't mean to spoil the

party!" He brushed away the past. "Didn't I smell something good?"

A feeling of relief swept through Twilight. She had lived so vividly the things Jingles described it seemed she had just returned from the long journey back to light. Some thought was pounding at her consciousness, but there was no time to examine it now. Busily she helped set out the many delicacies that had been made with such tender care and joy of sharing. Never had anything tasted so good as the wild blackberry tarts, the many cakes, pies, and cookies that she had to "take just a bite of, Miss Angel, and see if you want the recipe."

At last the evening was over. As she locked the door after everyone had helped clear away the remains, a feeling of love for these plain, honest folks swept through her. For a moment she hesitated before joining Aunt Lucy in the jeep with Jingles and the kids. This is my country, she thought, and the words in her mind seemed to sink deep into her heart and glow there like the bright star directly overhead. She was very quiet on the way home. Honey in her lap was asleep and Tommy was trying to keep awake. Aunt Lucy and Jingles were talking quietly together, leaving her to her own thoughts.

And once I thought my problems were

insurmountable, she mused, gazing out the frosty window at the world of white. Yet tonight I felt what real trouble is like. Yes, it's beautiful out there, but it could be cruel if you don't know how to cope with it. A wave of thankfulness threatened to overwhelm her, mingled with appreciation for the people who lived in this protean country. Somehow all the things she had once thought so important back in the city took on their proper perspective here.

Tonight there was no class distinction, no nightclubs, no fancy dresses, or hovering waiters. Yet when had she had a better time? Simplicity. That's the key. When Jeff and I are together again all I've learned here will help me be a better person. I don't think I could ever again be satisfied with a shallow, surface life. Not when I know what life can really be like. I will be a more understanding human being.

And never once did Twilight realize that in her newly perceptive state, she had changed the words "if we get together" to "when."

Chapter 8

Never had Twilight been busier than in the weeks between Thanksgiving and Christmas. In addition to the regular studies and papers to be checked, both the little one-room school and the local people were preparing for a Christmas Program. It had been decided to hold it in the old Golden West Lodge where church services were held rather than at the school. It was to be a gala affair — a potluck dinner for the entire community followed by THE PROGRAM. Everyone always thought of it as capitalized.

Twilight was amazed at the interest and excitement. Christmas Eve fell on Friday and the people who were having relatives from a distance had asked them to come early and enjoy the festivities. Although it was hard to keep their mind on studies, Twilight felt her pupils acquitted themselves quite well. In fact, they eagerly rushed through the regular classes in order to spend more time preparing for the Christmas Eve activity!

The walls of the little school were filled with

Christmas cards. For Art, Twilight had brought in a large packet of Christmas cards Aunt Lucy had received the year before. Each student chose one or more, and with colored paper, foil, bits of ribbons, crayons, and watercolors, made a duplicate to pin on the wall above the originals. Some of the cards were so well done it was next to impossible to discern which was the original from a distance. Twilight had gasped with amazement at Frank, Jr.'s, card — his choice of a scene with the Three Wise Men had been difficult to follow, but his inborn artistic ability had faithfully duplicated it. When Twilight saw the results she promptly put him in charge of scenery for the Christmas Eve program.

It had been decided to dismiss school at noon the day of Christmas Eve and take the students to decorate the old lodge. Red and green paper chains, carefully strung popcorn and cranberries, ornaments cut from old tin can tops, gilded nuts — all the things they could think of to make themselves now lay in boxes waiting to decorate the heavenly smelling large fir trees Cummings had cut and mounted in a stand for the church foyer. Twilight laughed at herself. Even though the old Golden West Lodge was just a big building, it was always called "church" by everyone. It was thrilling to see the children prepare for a real old-fashioned Christmas.

At last THE DAY came. Tired but happy, Twilight bundled into the waiting vehicles and herded her charges to their decorating project.

One by one they placed the ornaments on the great tree. The little ones did the lower branches, the big boys had brought a step-ladder, and it was Mike who finished off the tree with a great shining star. Standing back and looking at her happy students, Twilight had to admit that never had she seen a more beautiful or unusual tree. Yes, the decorations were all homemade, but they had been made with love. She smiled at the bobbing, delicate white snowflakes here and there on the tree. At the last minute little Tara Wilson had brought in a box of the dainty flakes.

"Why, what are these?" Twilight asked, holding them open with pleasure.

"Grandmother tatted them, then starched them," Tara explained shyly.

Indeed they were tatted, Twilight saw. They were also beautiful.

"Thank her for me," she told the little girl whose plain face glowed with praise at her contribution. Now they enhanced the tree with their paleness against the dark green branches.

It had been decided to start the evening

early as some of the folks had a long way to come. Miles Cummings had offered to drive out for Twilight and Aunt Lucy. He had recently purchased a new heavy pickup, equipping it against all weather.

"It will be more comfortable for Aunt Lucy," he told Twilight at the final community sing practice.

She smiled agreement. He was a nice person, and had been extremely helpful in arranging the singing. Unobtrusively offering assistance where needed, yet making sure things rolled along, he had helped Twilight screen the singers for those who could take special parts. Refusing to do a solo, he advised quietly, "Ask Jingles to sing 'O Holy Night.' "

Twilight promptly acted on his advice and was again amazed by the versatile talents of the weather-beaten friend who had helped her so much since that first day coming in on the *Lady of the Lake*. She had arranged it so he would sing the beautiful song a cappella just before the children's part of the program.

Her eye caught her mirrored reflection as she dressed in the warm red wool long dress she had packed in such haste those weeks ago. Pinning a bit of holly to her shoulder for color contrast, she remembered the day they had decided to vote on what kind of play to give.

"There are many things we could do," she

had told her eager students. "We could do Christmas from other lands, or a modern Christmas story or —" She was interrupted by the frantic waving of hands.

"Yes, Columbine?"

The girl's face was earnest. "Miss Angel, we want to do the real Christmas story." Every head nodded agreement. Twilight felt her heart swell within her.

"Very well," she told them quietly, turning away to hide the gathering mist in her eyes. Now she brushed that same mist from the eyes reflected in her mirror and smiled tremulously. She had learned so much more from her students than she could ever teach them!

"This is a night of double rejoicing," Aunt Lucy commented dryly as Twilight snuggled into her warm coat. "Glad I finally got that pesky cast off!"

Twilight laughed at her aunt. She was positively radiant tonight in a soft blue dress.

"Wait! I have just the thing to set off your dress!" Twilight dashed back into her own room for a moment. "There!" She settled a beautiful cross on a fine platinum chain over her aunt's head. The tiny diamond in the center sparkled in the firelight.

"Jeff gave it to me," she told her aunt.

Aunt Lucy looked at her fondly. "Twilight, you're healed. There was no trace of bitterness when you spoke of Jeff."

Twilight paused for a moment, then replied, "It's true, Aunt Lucy. Somehow up here in all this beauty I can't feel hardness toward anyone."

"Are you going to write to Jeff or Jenny?"

The girl reflected for a moment. "No, not yet. I want to give myself a little more time. Suppose I did and they were serious? I'm still not sure the hurt wouldn't come back. I'll wait until spring. That will give me a little more time."

Aunt Lucy said nothing, but the look she gave Twilight said volumes. Both knew Aunt Lucy's faith in Jeff and Jenny had never wavered, but she could appreciate Twilight's need to be sure of herself before meeting them.

Never had Twilight seen such an array of food as at that potluck supper! Chicken, beef, and venison flanked great bowls of potato, macaroni, and fruit salad. Mouth-watering varieties of cake, pie, and cookies. Homemade candy by the boxful. Piping hot vegetable casseroles, carefully reheated after their long trips through the cold evening. And the women! They kept plates filled, refilled, and filled again! But at last even the hungriest child could not fit in one more bite and things were cleared away. Silence descended after the noisy shuffling of chairs. It was time for THE PROGRAM.

For a moment Twilight's heart was too full for words as she gazed into the faces of her pupils, her neighbors, and her friends. But at last she spoke.

"You will never know what you have all done for me in the short time I've been with you. Words haven't been found to express the way I've come to appreciate you. So tonight all I can say from the bottom of my heart is — thank you." Before anyone could answer she announced,

"And now I give you — THE PROGRAM!"

From the first group singing of "Joy to the World," through the beautiful harmony of a medley of Christmas songs ranging from "Frosty, the Snowman" to "Silent Night," they sang. And how they sang! Quartets, groups, individuals — each one joyously participating. Applause. Laughter. Tears. And then it was time for the children's play.

"And it came to pass that in those days there went out a decree from Caesar Augustus that all the world should be taxed . . ." Mike Cummings's beautiful reading of the age-old Christmas story. Mary and Joseph, portrayed by Frank, Jr., and Columbine. Tommy, important as the hard-hearted innkeeper. "No room at the inn," he announced grandly.

But when "Away in the Manger" was sung, and the line came, "No crib for a bed," it was too much for little Pixie Jones. Leaving her place as an angel in the manger scene, she trotted to the sidelines where her baby brother's crib was, dragging it bumpity bump over the floor to the front.

"He can have my brother's," she told the astonished crowd. Quick as a flash dependable Frank, Jr., accepted as a true Joseph would have done.

"Thank you." He gently signaled to Mary, who carefully laid the big doll within the crib and tucked the blanket around it, then put her arm around Pixie.

Twilight held her breath. If anyone laughed it would spoil the entire play. She need not have worried. Miles Cummings had the shepherds all ready and as they immediately came to worship the newborn babe, Jingles softly started the beautiful old hymn "While Shepherds Watched their Flocks." Any emotion felt was swept away by the words of the song.

With the final song, and pronouncement of "Glory to God in the Highest and on Earth Peace, Good Will to Men," the play came to a triumphant end, but no one in the audience made a motion to go.

Questioningly, Twilight looked at them and reminded, "That concludes our Christmas Eve play. Thank you all for coming — and Merry Christmas!" but still no one moved.

Then from the back of the room Jingles's voice announced, "No, Miss Angel. It isn't quite over yet." Slowly he made his way forward, a gaily wrapped gift in his arms.

"It's from all of us — for you," he told the startled girl. She stared at him uncomprehendingly. Never had she dreamed such a thing, yet as she looked from face to face she could see they had all been in on the secret, from the smallest pupil to Grandma Wilson, who walked with a cane.

Jingles added a few words. "We are the ones to thank you for what you've brought to our students — and to ourselves."

Wonderingly Twilight opened the gift and held it up. It was a statue, perhaps twelve inches high, exquisitely wrought. An angel, wings tipped with gold. And with it a card: For our own Miss Angel.

It was too much. Twilight dropped her head in her hands and cried.

"Doesn't she like it, Grandpa?" Little Honey Jacobsen's troubled stage whisper sounded loud in the room, breaking the tension at Twilight's reaction. Lifting her face, her eyes shone through the sparkling tears.

"I love it!" She clutched the figurine tightly. "I have never had a present I like so well!"

Mike Cummings as usual had the last word. "Whew! Thought there for a minute we blew the whole thing!" Tears turned to laughter. Twilight set the angel on the piano for all to see and seized him in a big hug.

"Such grammar! Young man, it's a good thing we're out of school tonight. 'Blew it' indeed!" The entire group collapsed at her deliberate schoolteacher tone of voice, and under cover of the confusion of leaving Twilight managed to wipe away the tears and find her coat.

"I've never spent such a Christmas Eve," she confided to Aunt Lucy and Miles on the way home. "There was so much caring . . ."

"Isn't that what Christmas is really all about?" Miles asked quietly.

Twilight could only nod, while Aunt Lucy said nothing at all. She clutched within her the memory of Jingles's look as he wished her a very Merry Christmas. There had been caring in that look, too. But she would say nothing to Twilight. For now it was enough to know that the past was being healed in both of their lives, and that spring would come.

Chapter 9

For the first time since she had come to Stehekin Twilight was restless, moving from living room to bedroom, kitchen to porch, peering out the window. At last Aunt Lucy looked up from her sewing.

"Land sakes, Twilight, what's the matter with you?"

The girl dropped disconsolately into the big chair by the fire.

"I don't know," she confessed, rubbing her head. "Maybe I'm just tired." Aunt Lucy looked at her in concern.

"You aren't trying to come down with something, are you?"

"No, I just feel kind of tired and out of sorts." She poked at the fire. "I wish it would hurry up and get spring."

"You don't have to wait until spring to get out and enjoy the world," her aunt told her. "What's happened to Miles? For a while there in January it seemed like he was on the door-step constantly."

"He was." Her answer sounded abrupt

even in her own ears. Penitently she turned to her aunt. "I guess I just don't know how to handle men! First Jeff, now Miles."

"But I thought you liked him?"

"I do," she admitted unhappily. "He is a wonderful person. Maybe that's the trouble."

Her aunt laughed outright. "What's that supposed to mean?"

Twilight considered for a long time, then with sharp decision raised her chin. She had decided to tell Aunt Lucy the whole story.

"Miles is probably one of the finest men I will even know. But after he'd been coming around several times, I could see it wouldn't take much for him to start — to start liking me too much." She averted her gaze from Aunt Lucy's piercing look.

"And?"

"And I decided I wouldn't see him so much." She raised her head defiantly. "Maybe I'm crazy, but he reminds me so much of Jeff, and yet he isn't, and then . . ."

"Whoa! I get the picture. Did you tell Miles?"

Again the slender figure poked at the fire. "I didn't get the chance. The last time he brought me home I was so miserable wanting to level with him and being unsure how to start I acted so strange that he noticed. When he dropped me off he said he wouldn't be around for a while — too much paperwork to finish and so forth."

"And?" Aunt Lucy certainly wasn't making it easy.

"I said that would be fine with me. I was going to be pretty busy from now on too. Then I thanked him, oh, so politely for all the good times and came in the house. That was the last of January."

"And it's almost Valentine's day." Her aunt was silent so long Twilight wondered if she had fallen asleep, then she spoke.

"Twilight, I don't want to tell you what to do. Yet up here the rules are a little different than in the city. Everyone knows who is dating whom, and makes it a point to keep track. You wouldn't want to do anything to hurt Miles. If you get a chance, why don't you tell him pointblank how you feel? He would respect you a whole lot more than the way things are now."

"That's what I've been thinking," the girl admitted unhappily. "But he hasn't been back."

"Well, Valentine's Day is coming up and there's a big party at the Wilsons' that night. You'll see him then." It was all the consolation Aunt Lucy could give.

In the next few days Twilight brooded over what her wise aunt had said. Then a twinkle filled her eyes and when she left school a few days before the Valentine's party she carried with her extra bits and snips of paper, lace, and a felt-tip pen. She was going to send a valentine. Her pupils had been too busy making their own valentines for one another and for their school valentine party to notice her activities.

Later that night she surveyed the comic valentine she had turned out and propped it on her dresser. She almost wanted to show it to Aunt Lucy but, still giggling, she decided to wait. She would leave it on the dresser and when her aunt came in to dust, as she persisted in doing over Twilight's continued protest, she would see it.

Aunt Lucy chuckled and chuckled the next day. Someone was in for a real surprise when that card was received! She could hardly wait to see what repercussions it caused.

Valentine's Day fell on a Friday and Twilight's classes were rapidly finished so there would be plenty of time for the party. As it turned out, there was a valentine for each one in the school from each of the others! Some were elaborate affairs such as the beautiful "store-boughten" ones Columbine received from both Mike and Frank, Jr. Others were the result of hours of painstaking labor. Again, the artwork of some were outstanding examples of what creative minds could do with a little bit of encouragement.

Aunt Lucy and Twilight had stayed up late the night before baking not only a huge valentine cake, but also valentine cookies that the pupils could carry home. Molasses, in the shape of big hearts, they were both delicious and attractive, with their funny frosting faces peering up inviting that first bite. It was a happy group of young people who left school that evening, calling back gay greetings and "see you tomorrow nights."

Valentine's Day had arrived somewhere else, too. At the National Park Service headquarters an envelope addressed in an unfamiliar female hand had been delivered to Mike Cummings along with the rest of his mail. Half disturbed at what it might contain, he waited until he was alone during the lunch break to open it.

A shout of laughter issued from his office — it was just as well no one was there to hear. Grinning broadly, he leaned back to survey the unexpected card in his hand.

Against a group of hastily sketched green trees the face of a squirrel peered out. On the front of the card were the words —

"If friends like you . . ."

On the second fold of the tri-fold card was a wrinkled, scarred walnut, also bearing a face, and written below —

". . . grew on trees . . ."

And when he opened up the last fold there was a snapshot of Aunt Lucy's little log house, complete with Twilight laughing on the porch, surrounded by its background of woods, and at the bottom the final caption —

". . . I'd move to the forest!"

There was no signature; none was needed to identify the artist. Still chuckling, Miles tucked the card in his jacket pocket and with a wicked gleam in his eyes scribbled a note telling the office staff he would be out for a little bit. When he returned from his errand several people noticed the sly grin still on his face but no one knew of the box he had carefully procured, wrapped in a bit of leftover Christmas tissue, and tied with a clumsy red bow. I'll really surprise her, he thought to himself, and somehow the bit of nonsense brightened the rest of the rather drab February day.

That evening Twilight and Aunt Lucy were busy before the fire when Jingles dropped by for a moment, carrying a package.

"For you, Miss Angel. Fellow in town asked me to drop it off."

She wonderingly held up the box. It rattled. What on earth . . . ? She was almost afraid to open it before Jingles, but there was nothing else to do. She untied the ribbon hesitantly. No tag, no identification. Could Jeff . . . ? She disciplined the thought almost before it was born. Then the box was open. Jingles stared in disgust.

"A box of walnuts? Who'd send a valentine like that?" He paused for a moment. "Well, takes all kinds, I guess." Striding to the door, a slight tinge of red crept under his clear tan skin.

"This is more my idea of a valentine." He awkwardly held out from behind him a huge box of candy, pink ribbons, lace and all, to Aunt Lucy, who dropped her sewing and beamed.

"Thank you, Jake." There was a suspicious moisture in her blue eyes and immediately Jingles grew uncomfortable.

"I have to be going. See you all tomorrow night," and he was out the door before either of the women could say another word.

"Well! A valentine for each of us!" Aunt Lucy chuckled, but there was a tenderness in her eyes.

"I didn't dare look at you when I opened that box of nuts," Twilight confessed. "If I had known I would have laughed and given the whole thing away. But I could hardly keep a straight face when I saw that box of walnuts! Miles must have really thought to come up with such a unique way of responding to my card. Now I feel we can be friends again. And this time," she added resolutely, "I intend to have that talk with him before there is any more uncomfortable feeling on either part."

"It's going to be sooner than you think," Aunt Lucy predicted wisely. "Listen." The sound of a motor stopping in front of the house had alerted her. Over Twilight's protests she snatched her box of candy and headed for her own room.

"I'm sure he didn't come to see me," she told her niece. "Get it taken care of, then when you're through talking tap on my door and ask me if I'm through with my room cleaning and I'll come out."

"You old fraud," Twilight accused. "You cleaned that room yesterday!"

"You know that and I know that but Miles doesn't," Aunt Lucy announced smugly. "Go answer the door," and she vanished through her bedroom doorway.

A small smile at her aunt's duplicity still lingered on Twilight's face as she opened the door to Miles, but all she said was, "Thank you for the nuts. I know Aunt Lucy and I will both enjoy them."

Miles laughed at her demure manner, then after a quick look to see that Aunt Lucy wasn't about he sobered and told Twilight, "I was glad to get your card. The last time we were together I felt that in some way I had done something to offend you. Couldn't for the life of me figure what it was, but I'm glad whatever it was seems to be cleared up."

Twilight shook her head. "You hadn't offended me, Miles. It's just that . . ." Her voice trailed off, then, gripping her courage with both hands, she plunged in.

"I just don't want you to like me too much." Taking silence for disagreement, she blundered on nervously.

"I like you, Miles, I like you a great deal. But that's all that it can ever be. Just like." Controlling the tremor in her voice, she sketched in her love for Jeff, omitting any mention of Jenny, but finishing with the fact they had quarreled and she had run away.

"But you're still in love with him." Put flatly, she could only agree. Then Miles did the last thing she would have expected. He laughed. Not a little polite laugh of understanding, not a sarcastic laugh, but a big hearty shoulder-shaking laugh that filled the house, causing Aunt Lucy in her room to pause and wonder.

"I fail to see anything funny about what I said," Twilight told him icily, cheeks burning. She had needed all the strength she had to talk with him that way, and all he did was laugh! At last, seeing she was really upset, Miles's laughter ceased and he wiped the tears of mirth from his eyes.

"I'm sorry, Angel," he told her, but there was still a twinkle of mischief in his eyes so like his son Mike when he had pulled a joke in school. He saw she didn't believe him and this did more to settle him down than anything else. Taking both her hands in his, he became deadly serious.

"I wouldn't do anything in the world to hurt your feelings. You are a very special person, and I am glad to have you for my friend. Yes," he emphasized, "my friend." Even as he looked at her, Twilight could tell his thoughts were far away. With a visible effort he returned to the present, noticed he still held her hands, and dropped them.

"It's been a joy to take you places, Angel," he told her seriously. "Yes, it's been lonely for us since my wife died. Then, too, a widower is prey to well-meaning relatives and friends who just happen to know 'this marvelous single female friend' and want to introduce her." He crossed to the window, looking out into the night.

"No one could ever take my wife's place. If others wish to remarry that is fine for them, but for me it wouldn't be enough. Our marriage was a unity that could not be matched, or replaced. That's why I liked you, Angel. . . . Even though nothing was said, I could tell you weren't interested in a big romance. I guessed the reason last fall when I noticed the whiter band on your ring finger, a telltale sign of recent engagement, or even marriage. I felt comfortable with you — until you started acting a little strangely. I didn't know quite how to put you at ease, even though I guessed what might be bothering you. Maybe I would have guessed wrong — how could I ask and reassure you? You have nothing to fear from me, *tillicum*."

It was a long speech for Miles and Twilight could feel the effort it had cost him to make it, but miraculously the air was cleared. She smiled at him.

"Then there's no reason why we can't go on being friends? I remember when I first came to Stehekin Jingles told me *tillicum* meant friend. That's what you mean, isn't it, Miles?"

In a twinkling Miles's serious mood changed to teasing. "It sure is," he drawled. "I calkilate as how if I drag you around it will keep all them thar widder wimmin from a-trailin' me."

Twilight laughed until she couldn't sit up straight at his foolishness, and at her own. How could she have mistaken his real friendship for anything deeper? He was so like his son, and they had both accepted her as she was, asking no more than she could give. A voice from the doorway recalled her to the fact that Aunt Lucy was standing there with a broad grin, extending her box of candy as an offering.

"I couldn't help overhearing Twilight's laugh," she apologized. "So I figured it was safe to come out." Amid the noisy evening that followed there was no time for reflection, and it wasn't until Miles left that Twilight could sort out all the emotions she had experienced that evening. Fear of speaking, embarrassment, humiliation, all turned into a sense of peace and rightness.

"I could have cheerfully killed him," she told Aunt Lucy. "When he laughed I was tempted to take the poker to him. But then I realized it was the best thing he could have done. If he had protested, I would have gone on feeling he really did care and was trying to cover up. Even though it was dreadful to be laughed at, it convinced me. No one even slightly in love with a woman could laugh at her like that!"

Aunt Lucy did some laughing of her own. "Also, he made you laugh at yourself," she pointed out. "That's always good for all of us."

Twilight nodded. "Yes, if you can learn to laugh at yourself and your mistakes first, then it will never matter if everyone else laughs because you've already accepted them personally."

"You know, Twilight," her aunt commented, "with those comments I really feel there's hope for you."

Twilight caught the approving tone behind her aunt's mocking words.

"You mean for me — a city slicker?" she imitated Miles's drawl perfectly. "Well, in that case, I calkilate as how I'll go to bed!"

She thought of the moment on her way to school the next week and how she really was learning to accept herself enough to laugh and admit she had been in the wrong. It helped her through a rather dreary Monday. After the excitement of Valentine's Day, and the Saturday evening party where she had noticed the glances of approval at her and Miles, it was hard for everyone to settle back in school routine. The students seemed to feel it too and for the first time she had to correct some of them for whispering.

That evening she told Aunt Lucy about her day. "I don't know what would have become of all of us if Mike hadn't provided a laugh. We were all kind of letdown, nothing seemed new and fresh. Even the snow is kind of dirty and unattractive around the schoolyard. It's too cold to be outside for noon games and boring indoors. Then Mike provided such a diversion I didn't even have the heart to scold him."

"What happened?" Aunt Lucy wanted to know. It was the first time Twilight had mentioned discipline problems and she was curious to know how "Miss Angel" had handled them.

"You know how I set up a rule that personal items such as lunches, balls, and so forth had to be kept on the big shelf at the back of the room instead of in the desks?"

Her aunt nodded. "Yes, you told me how things were always rolling out and disturbing class. Didn't you tell your students that anything that was kept in a desk that rolled out automatically became your property?"

"Yes, that was the only way to stop the everlasting clutter and noise. Anyway, today Mike had about the biggest, shiniest red apple you could imagine. He hated to part with it, and I noticed he slipped it in his desk when he thought I wasn't watching. Everything was fine until just before Social Studies. He went to take out his book and out came the apple, plunk, plunk, plunk, right down the aisle." She grinned in remembrance of the looks of the other students.

"And then?" Aunt Lucy relied on one of her favorite expressions.

"And then, before I could say a word, the young scamp grabbed the apple, brushed it off on his shirt, and came to my desk with this angelic smile that fooled no one. 'Here, Miss Angel, this is for you,' and laid it on my desk. He knew it was mine anyway, but had to forestall comment so he brought it up as a gift!"

Aunt Lucy laughed until she cried. "Sounds familiar. What did you do with the apple?"

"Well, I laughed along with the rest of the class and thanked him politely. Then after school I returned it with the warning that from now on all apples were to be considered the same as the other contraband for desks and he would be expected to keep them elsewhere."

"Good for you! There's a time for rules and a time for flexibility. I'm glad to see you're learning when to bend."

"I didn't have the heart to keep it," Twilight explained. "Not after his rescuing us from sheer boredom. Seems like I'm all out of inventive ideas for a while. As soon as the weather is nicer I'm going to do nature hikes and some field trips. But right now all we have to look forward to is the usual battery of achievement tests! I dread those. What if my students do poorly? You know I have to sign that we didn't have prior classwork geared to the tests, and after I give them they are sent away for machine scoring. I've really tried to teach my best, but how will their scores compare? Maybe we've been emphasizing the wrong things entirely and the test results will show it!" She moved restlessly to the window again.

"Sit down, you make me nervous with your prowling. Your students will do just fine. If you think it's bad for you, what about the days when you had to put your students through eighth-grade exams? They were given by the state. You weren't even allowed to administer them to your own classes. A state person came in, gave the tests, took them away and scored them, and results came back as to whether your students had been successful. If they hadn't, you had better start looking for another job. It was a big criteria as to how good a teacher was. That, and if all your first graders were able to read by the end of the year and read well."

Twilight gasped. "How could anyone do it?"

A reminiscent look filled Aunt Lucy's eyes. "They did it. For one thing, reading was taught differently. From the first day of school until Thanksgiving first graders worked with phonics charts. They learned their sounds in every combination imaginable. No books were issued until between Thanksgiving and Christmas, and when they got their first readers at that time, they could sound out the words and in most cases, make a pretty fair showing of themselves."

"I can agree with that," Twilight replied. "I know that in my first grade we had phonics, even some in kindergarten. Now it's easy for me to sound out even unfamiliar words, and to be a good speller. Jenny was taught by the sight method, and while she's a good reader, her spelling is atrocious, and she'd probably spell it a-t-r-o-s-h-u-s!"

They both laughed at her nonsense, but Aunt Lucy went on.

"When I see the teacher strikes and the negotiations that aren't settled and the school closures, I wonder how much modern education has improved. It's the students who are hurt when there are no classes. We learn to love our work and our students, even as I think you are doing here, Twilight."

"Yes, I am." There was a curious stillness in the girl and a question in her eyes. "Aunt Lucy, will I be finishing out the year with my students?"

"Do you want to?" her aunt asked quietly.

There was no hesitation in Twilight's answer. "Very much. At first it was enough just to help out, but now I'd like to finish what I've started. Especially with Columbine, Mike, and Frank, Jr. They are leaving the one-room school this year and I'd hate for them to have to get used to another teacher just for a few months."

"I think it can be arranged," Aunt Lucy said, her eyes twinkling. "I understand the school board hasn't been overwhelmed with applications for the rest of the term." Her smile gave her away.

"How hard did they look?" Twilight demanded.

All her aunt would say was "Not too hard," but it spoke volumes. It signified faith and trust in her the community had shared, even more than she had had in herself, Twilight realized.

"I'm glad," she confessed, shamefaced, but Aunt Lucy put her at ease.

"They wanted *you*, honey," she reassured.

"It's quite a responsibility, isn't it?" Twilight said

"Yes. When parents send their children to school they are entrusting their most priceless possessions for the better part of those children's waking hours to another. The children will look to their teacher for much more than 'book learning.' I don't know of anyone who is more responsible morally for the safety, guidance, and education of children than a dedicated teacher. I'm glad you've sensed that."

Hours later Twilight tossed and turned in bed as she thought of Aunt Lucy's words. "Most priceless possessions . . . morally responsible . . . dedicated teacher." She thought of Aunt Lucy's years of service and marveled. She could have very well been describing herself, Twilight thought, yet how she would ridicule the thought! Aunt Lucy was not the conceited type. She saw her duty and did it, and that was the way it was. Smiling, Twilight heard the sound of wind in the trees.

"Spring is on its way," she whispered to herself, and a fierce joy shot through her. Somehow with the coming of spring, all her problems would be worked out. They had to. How could anyone feel depressed or miserable or at odds with the world when spring came? Not me, she thought. I can't wait for spring. By then I'll be completely healed and ready to face whatever might come. Aunt Lucy said she had planted bulbs last fall and they are dormant in the ground through the frozen winter. But with the first sunshine and warm spring rain they will spring up. Crocus, daffodils, heralds of a rebirth. I'm like that, too. All winter the seeds of faith have been lying dormant, yet working within themselves like Aunt Lucy's bulbs. Soon they will come to life again.

I'm not the same person I was last fall, she mused. It was worth all the pain to learn the lessons Stehekin has taught me. I came up here in search of myself, in search of Twilight. I've found it. Stehekin — the way through. Like Aunt Lucy I'm nearing the end of my dark tunnel. There's nothing but light and sunshine ahead . . . and spring.

Chapter 10

Spring had come to Stehekin. Birds proclaimed it in their throaty songs. Pussy-willows along the creek banks shouted it. Students on their way to school expressed it as they skirted puddles of shining water or gleefully plowed through them, depending on their age. Every branch and limb were budding and newly washed green. Along the shady slopes wild trilliums, wood violets, Johnny jump-ups, and bleeding heart were carefully searched out to make their way into overflowing vases of flowers into the one-room school. Even Miss Angel was different. Her pupils couldn't explain it — they had always almost worshipped her but with spring had come a new softness. Her beautiful face had never been more aglow. They saw — and wondered.

"She's in love," Columbine whispered to Frank, Jr., who had been doing some longing-filled looking at Columbine herself.

"Uh-huh," he agreed absently, wondering why Columbine was getting prettier all the time, never realizing it was because he was growing up to appreciate girls more than when he was younger.

Columbine smiled to herself. Not for the world would she have said anything to anyone but Frank, Jr. She had it all figured out that Miss Angel and Miles Cummings were a couple. There had been a time when she thought they were angry with each other, but not now. It's the only thing that could make a woman look like that, Columbine thought with a moment of rare understanding for an eighth-grade girl. I wonder if I will be like her? It was already decided that Columbine would go to Chelan next fall for high school, along with Frank, Jr., and Mike Cummings. Knowing that all three of them would be together through the week made it easier to be gone, and who knew — perhaps in time . . . but at this point Columbine always blushed to herself furiously and turned her thoughts elsewhere.

Spring had arrived almost overnight. One day there were still great patches of snow dotting the landscape like feather pillows, the next they were gone. Twilight had awakened to the sound of wind in what she tended to call "her trees" outside her bedroom window. There was a strange sound in it, almost a whine. Not a cold, piercing wind, but one that was warm and mellow.

"It's the chinook," Aunt Lucy explained.

"Chinook? You mean the wind?"

"Yes. When that certain warm wind comes after winter, taking with it the remainder of the snow and bringing new life to the land, it is the chinook. Chinook is an Indian word, I don't know what it means. But that's what this particular wind is called."

Twilight tucked the bit of information into her growing store of nature lore and that day they discussed it in school. She was amazed to find that even the smallest pupils knew all about it! Round eyes shining, it was little Tara Wilson, the lover of beauty who told Twilight how they all looked forward to the chinook and the end of winter.

Honey Jacobsen chimed in with, "Yes, Miss Angel. And Grandpa takes Tommy and me down to the river to see it."

"The river?" Again Twilight was puzzled.

Tommy took up the story, very man-of-the-world in his explanation to "teacher." "Yes, he does. Every year since we've been here. It's really something to see. Could we go, Miss Angel? Could we go?"

"I'll have to see."

She postponed decisions until after checking with Aunt Lucy, but the next day announced, "On Friday, bring extra warm clothes and a bigger lunch. We're going on a field trip." Shouts of excitement greeted her statement, and she was glad she had waited until the end of the day to make her announcement. Jingles had been over the night before and had smilingly agreed to chaperone the group. He would bring his truck, and all could crowd into it. The students respected him; there would be no trouble with him at the helm of their expedition.

Thursday raced by. Twilight had long since learned the easiest way to keep her pupils' interest was to relate studies to life right here in Stehekin. What had at first amazed her, the loyal, almost fierce pride in their country, was now accepted as part of her students and put to good use. Now she held a discussion on explorers, likening their trip to an exploration. They talked about Columbus, and Madame Curie, and Kit Carson. They touched on Lewis and Clark, and Einstein, and John Glenn. Each had been an explorer. Today was a time for thinking about what they would find on their own venture.

Friday dawned crisp and beautiful, and Twilight was glad for the stocking cap and extra sweater Aunt Lucy had insisted she wear. Instead of accompanying them, Aunt Lucy would meet them for lunch, bringing a kettle of hot soup, one of chocolate, and a homemade cake. It would be a surprise for everyone and a welcome addition to the lunches the children would bring.

What a day! Twilight felt her heart bursting with pride, curiosity, and something as old as age itself, that inborn gladness that spring had come. It was only a few weeks until Easter, which fell late this year. Her pupils were equally eager, partly because for the first time they were to be teachers, she the pupil. It was for them to show her the nooks where they had found the beautiful flowers they brought her. It was for them to seek out with newly appreciative eyes the beauty of the surrounding area, seeing it as she saw it, loving it for its familiarity, yet noticing things they had not particularly paid attention to before but were now anxious to share with Miss Angel. Each separate bird, flower, or tree had to be carefully examined. They marveled at the great eagle who perched high above, disdainfully surveying their group, at last swooping through the sky to leave them staring at him. They had studied his habits and why he had been chosen the national bird. They appreciated his soar to freedom.

But of all the things they saw, nothing impressed Twilight as much as the rivers and streams. Those tiny brooks and larger waterways had doubled and tripled, seemingly overnight. The chinook wind had released snow in the mountains and the spring runoff was in full force.

"It's unbelievable!" Twilight stared, feeling popeyed at the sight of the formerly peaceful, then icebound river now carrying great sections of logs, uprooted trees, and debris, turned into a brown monster devouring the very banks on which they once stood.

"It's dangerous," Jingles warned the group, especially Miss Angel. The others had lived in the mountains long enough to fully respect such a sight and keep back, but in her eagerness Twilight would have gone to the very brink, never realizing how the angry waters had cut underneath, leaving only a protruding shelf along the bank that could split, crumbled, into the seething water.

Jingles provided an invaluable service. There were questions Twilight couldn't have begun to answer, but his ready wit and patient understanding of spring and children soon evidenced in the way he was bombarded with their queries. He loved it. The fact that he had deep feelings for the country only added to his information. Twilight felt the group probably learned more about natural science that day than in the entire study session she had given on wild and growing things!

"Wait until summer," the Richards twins promised. "We'll take you berrying." As usual Pam assumed the lead by adding, "I know the best places to get the most and biggest berries."

Penny solemnly nodded. "Yes, she does. But she also eats as many as she puts in her bucket!"

Twilight laughed outright, promising to go, then a sudden thought struck her, leaving a pang. Would she be here in the summertime? Would she see this protean land flow from spring to summer to fall? Refusing to think of the future, she turned toward the road where Aunt Lucy's jeep was manfully struggling with ruts created by soft ground and mud. The main road was farther over, this was a little more out of the way. To Twilight's horror, she saw that Aunt Lucy seemed powerless to control the jeep. It was heading down a gentle slope straight for the eddying brown river! She glimpsed her aunt's white face and caught the words "brakes" as the determined woman feebly tried to halt the onrushing vehicle.

"Jingles!" Twilight's scream cut the air, stopping him in his tracks near the river where he had been showing Columbine a chattering squirrel in the tree above. In a glance he took in the situation.

"Lucy!" His bellow was heard even above the noise of the river and the jeep.

"Turn left!" Nodding imperceptibly, Aunt Lucy jerked the wheel, managing to turn the jeep away from the raging waters, but a group of evergreen growing close together swallowed up the jeep as she plunged into them with a crackle of branches and breaking limbs.

Twilight found herself running as she had never run before. Fear lent wings to her feet. Not Aunt Lucy, she sobbed, unaware she had spoken aloud, trying to keep up with her students. She hadn't realized the depth of her feelings for this beloved aunt before. Part of her mind was racing ahead, unwillingly bracing herself for what she might find. But in spite of even her eighth-grade boys' fleetness of foot, it was Jingles who first crashed into the thicket of trees.

"Thank God!" They heard his words even before he appeared in the opening where the jeep had torn through, coming to rest against one big tree. He held Aunt Lucy tight in his arms, as if he would never let her go. She was scratched and bruised, one shoe was gone, one arm had a long scratch, but she smiled faintly at the group.

"More than one way to get attention." It was too much for Twilight. Stumbling to a big rock, she dropped down next to her aunt.

"I thought you were killed," she wailed, not heeding the scared looks of her students.

"Just my jeep." The dryness of Aunt Lucy's tone did more to restore Twilight's balance than anything else could have done.

"What a woman," she announced to the little group of onlookers. "I suppose she thinks this is all part of living here in Stehekin!"

"That's what she thinks," Jingles growled. He had lived through eons of time from that moment he had seen Aunt Lucy plunging toward the death currents of that wild river until he had found her sitting dazed, but not really hurt, in the jeep. Not caring that there was an audience of eleven delighted onlookers, he held her firmly and announced to her and the world at large, "I'm sick and tired of you trying to take care of yourself. If you aren't too proud to have a guide for a husband, my place is waiting for you."

Aunt Lucy put her head down and cried. There was stunned silence on the part of the group. Didn't she want to marry Jingles? Honey Jacobsen saved the day.

"We want you to marry us." She patted Aunt Lucy's hair, now tousled from her recent experience. "Grandpa, and Tommy, and me. We want you to marry us."

Aunt Lucy's blue eyes looked into Honey's own. Tears still flowed down her cheeks, but she put her arms around Honey, drawing her close into the circle she and Jingles made, motioning for Tommy to join them.

"I'd be happy to marry you all," she told them brokenly.

Twilight came to her senses suddenly and turned to her other students, who were gazing with delighted grins at the little family-to-be.

"Come on," she beckoned gaily, pointing to the trampled path the jeep had made. "Let's see if there's anything left of the lunch Aunt Lucy had in the jeep!" Followed by her entire school with the exception of Tommy and Honey, she made her way to the battered Jeep.

"Aw, it isn't so bad," Mike pronounced, backed up by Frank, Jr.'s.

"Yeah. The front part is bent but Dad and Jingles can fix that. Her jeep will be good as new." Twilight could sense the relief in their manner to get away from the more sentimental scene just witnessed. But Pixie Jones wasn't so easily distracted.

"Are they going to get married, Miss Angel?" Others took up the question. "Are they?" "Are they?"

"Yes," Twilight told them. "Yes, they are." Her simple acceptance of the proposal seemed to satisfy most of them, but when they were unpacking the slightly tattered lunch Aunt Lucy had brought, it was Rusty Jones who voiced the question all of them were wondering.

"Jingles said, 'Thank God.' Miss Angel, did God really keep Aunt Lucy from going into the river?"

A few months before Twilight wouldn't have been able to answer the question as she now did, simply and unhesitatingly. She had believed in God, but this land of surprises had taught her to rely on Him more than she had back in Seattle. Now she told Rusty, and the others whose busy hands had paused for her answer,

"Yes, Rusty, He did."

"I'm glad." Twilight was surprised to see tears shine in Pam Richard's eyes. "I love Aunt Lucy."

"Me, too," Penny echoed, and the others nodded even though the big boys looked embarrassed. Jingles's voice broke the little silence.

"Where's dinner? I'm starved!" His welcome shout released them all from the moment of serious sharing, but Twilight knew it was only another pearl to add to her ever-growing string of memories that were weaving a necklace of her first year in teaching.

The rest of the afternoon flew. Because of Aunt Lucy's accident Twilight had wanted to postpone the rest of the day's field trip.

"Not on my account," Aunt Lucy told them. "There's a blanket in the truck and I'll be perfectly comfortable. You go ahead and look around." Her total acceptance of things as they were encouraged Twilight to go on, but before long her students were ready to call it quits. It had been an eventful day, and the lunch and warm sun did their work. They were full and a little tired and rather quiet as they headed back. Each of them had in turn admired the simple ring now on Aunt Lucy's finger. It didn't look new, and Twilight wondered if it could possibly be the one Aunt Lucy had worn so many years ago. She asked that evening, and her aunt met her gaze directly.

"Yes, Twilight. Jingles said when we parted he couldn't bear to throw away the ring or sell it so he put it away in a safe deposit box. Years passed and when he came up here, he took his personal effects from the box and there it was. He had it cleaned and has carried it in his pocket ever since, not really hoping, just as a reminder of happy days. Now it's come home."

"Come home." Twilight echoed her aunt's words, thinking to herself, All those years, he waited. So did she. Now they can be happy, and make others happy. She thought of the way Honey and Tommy had announced to all that afternoon "She won't be Aunt Lucy pretty soon. She'll be Grandma!"

They would be a good family, that Twilight knew. Not afraid to discipline the children, yet surrounding them with so much love that even discipline could be accepted as part of life. Again Twilight thought, as she had so many times since leaving Seattle, I hope I can grow up to be just like Aunt Lucy, never realizing she was well on the way.

"Would you like to stay here in the log cabin or come with us?" Aunt Lucy asked.

"My goodness, I'd never thought of that!" Twilight gasped, then asked quickly, "Won't you be selling this place?"

"No, sir!" Her aunt's response was quick and to the point. "Too many good memories here. We'll keep it and use it for a treat when things at the guide service get too much. It will be a good weekend hideout in time."

"Then I'd like to stay," Twilight confessed. "I have a lot of good memories here, too." Her eyes wandered dreamily around the room, to the fireplace, the shining windows, the little porch.

"Good." Her aunt's tone smacked of satisfaction. "We didn't want to leave it empty, but if you'd been afraid to live by yourself . . ."

Twilight shook her head. "I've never been afraid here, except of bears," she amended hastily.

Aunt Lucy laughed outright. "Haven't seen one since that one." She nudged the great skin on the floor, while Twilight shivered at the remembrance of how it came to be there. "Besides, Tommy is going to teach you to shoot. You'll have no problem."

Twilight thought of her aunt's words in the next few weeks. True to her promise, Tommy was teaching her to shoot. To her own surprise, she found she had a natural ability with a rifle. Jingles provided one that wasn't too heavy, and before long Twilight was quite a markswoman. She had every tree around riddled with holes where she had practiced on the ringed targets Tommy set up for her and the day came when he pronounced her "better than I am." She only laughed at that. Tommy was an outstanding shot for a boy his age, better than most of the men. But his praise did her good, and a warm glow shot through her that this, the first of her students she had met so long ago, would be such a faithful, loyal friend.

The whole community was excited over Jingles and Aunt Lucy's approaching wedding. After waiting so long, they had decided not to postpone their happiness any longer than necessary. The wedding was set for Easter Sunday afternoon.

"No fuss and feathers," Aunt Lucy said. "But somehow Easter is such a special time for new beginnings, a new life." Twilight agreed. Easter this year would indeed be a new experience for her. Starting with a 6:00 A.M. community Easter Sunrise Service, followed by a potluck breakfast, a preaching service including several special Easter musical numbers and featuring Jingles singing "The Holy City," that afternoon the wedding would be a wonderful way to cap the day and start anew. Twilight vaguely remembered attending a sunrise service once long ago with some friends, but she couldn't have told exactly what it was that had caused her to remember. She eagerly anticipated the services in this beautiful unspoiled place.

"I wish Jenny could be here," she said aloud, failing to notice Aunt Lucy's guilty start as she went on rolling cookie dough. "I'm going to write to her Sunday afternoon. Easter would be a beautiful time for me to apologize for running away."

"That would be nice." Aunt Lucy's voice sounded choked, but then she was leaning over the stove taking cookies from the oven and that probably explained it.

Saturday afternoon Twilight, her students, and Miles Cummings banked flowers everywhere imaginable at the old Golden West Lodge. It was a big job, but one filled with love. Honey and Tommy strutted around, importantly giving orders, pronouncing how they got to "stand up with Grandpa and Aunt Lucy," and generally getting in everyone's way.

"Funny," Twilight told Miles as he drove her home through the gathering dusk. "You'd think those two had engineered the whole thing!" Miles laughed in agreement.

"They sure are happy." Both fell silent, appreciating the beauty of the evening.

"If I ever get married and have a girl I am going to name her April Twilight. It's my favorite month, my favorite time of day."

Miles looked at her with fondness. Since the open declaration of friendship they had grown to be companions, loving one another without being in love at all, content just to share and explore together without strain on each part.

"You're quite a girl, Angel," he told her, waving as she ran up the walk to Aunt Lucy's porch. She turned, smiled in return, and a trace of the smile still lingered as she flung open the door.

"It's decorated beautifully, Aunt Lucy,"

she called, but stopped short at the sight of the girl standing by the fireplace. A girl she knew, but didn't know. A girl with brown glowing hair, brown eyes now a little hesitant. A girl whose face showed she had passed through suffering, yet held a strength Twilight had never before seen. For a moment she clutched the door frame, unable to believe her own eyes. Then with a rush of emotion she opened her arms wide.

"Jenny, oh, Jenny, it's really you!" With a slight sob the smaller girl ran to her, tears spilling over, crying again and again,

"Twilight, I've found you! Thank God, I've found you!"

Chapter 11

"Why didn't you tell us?" the girls accused Aunt Lucy reproachfully. Her answer was typical.

"Thought you'd be more natural if you didn't know." She chuckled. "It worked, too, didn't it!" Twilight and Jenny both had to laugh. The first minutes after Twilight had come in had cleared away the doubts of months. Now hastily excusing herself on some pretense, Twilight hurried to the porch and gave way to tears. She was so caught up in her own grief she failed to hear soft footsteps approaching. The touch of a small hand on her shoulder recalled her to the present.

"I will never forgive myself!" she sobbed, a fresh wave of misery enveloping her at the thought of Jenny going into the hospital all alone while she had run away from something that didn't even exist.

"Nonsense!" Aunt Lucy had briskly stepped up behind Jenny. "You thought and did what most of us would have done in like circumstances. Don't waste more of your time regretting that which you can't change. You can't live it again. Besides —" She hesitated, almost unwilling to say what she felt necessary. "If you hadn't misconstrued the situation, you would never have learned the lessons Stehekin has taught you."

"That's right," Jenny chimed in. "Even though it was hard, Twilight, it helped me be a total person myself. I've always gone to you with everything. This time I had Jeff and the Matthewsons, but most of all I had to rely on myself. I determined to get so well you would be proud of me when I found you."

Twilight stared at her younger sister in astonishment. Never had she been so positive. The few months since they had been together had done something to Jenny.

"Why, Jenny, you're a woman!" she blurted out, amazed at her own discovery. It was true. She had left an eager but quiet girl. Before her stood a radiant young woman, not a carbon copy of Twilight, but a person in her own right. A strange pang of regret mixed with anticipation thrilled Twilight. No longer just "younger sister," Jenny would be more of a companion in the future.

"But what are your plans?" Aunt Lucy wanted to know. In the confusion of greetings little had been said of the future.

"I'm all set for nursing school in the fall."

Jenny positively glowed. "Tests, physical, everything is all out of the way. So until then I thought maybe you could put up with me?" There was a twinkle in the beautiful brown eyes and Twilight couldn't resist hugging her sister again.

"Of course! It's perfect! I can finish out my teaching —"

She was interrupted by Jenny's round-eyed question, "*You're teaching?* But the paper said the teacher was a Miss Angel." Seeing Twilight's mischievous grin, she said, "Miss Angel. Angelical Aha, methinks I see your fine crafty hand. Was it part of the disappearing act?"

Twilight had the grace to blush. Her running away now seemed such a silly, childish act. Aunt Lucy came to her rescue.

"Come back inside where it's warmer." Leading them to the fire, she matter-of-factly explained how Twilight had gained the nickname Miss Angel. Jenny went pale during the story of the bear, but pride shone in her face at the rest of the tale. In the reflective silence that fell, it was Aunt Lucy who asked the question on Twilight's mind.

"Jenny, what about Jeff?" She had no need to elaborate. Jenny knew what she meant.

"I don't know." Her reply was honest, but she carefully avoided looking at Twilight.

"He was terribly hurt that Twilight hadn't trusted him. But lately he hasn't mentioned it. A few times I've tried to bring it up and he only smiled a little sadly, then changed the subject. I just don't know." Her words hung in the air. Twilight felt as if she had been dealt a physical blow. She could see her own actions through Jeff's eyes, and in their light, what she had done appeared to be mountainous. Would he ever forgive her? But tonight was no time to brood.

"Jenny." She deliberately pushed back hovering tears and made her voice bright. "I'll bet you don't even know there's to be a wedding in the family tomorrow!" Her sister saw the effort she made and matched her own tone.

"Oh, yes, I do! You didn't know I arrived shortly after you went to decorate. Good thing I allowed extra time for my letter — Aunt Lucy only received it yesterday, but her bridegroom was right on hand when the ferry docked today. By the way" — she turned to Aunt Lucy with a very sincere look — "he seems like a wonderful person. I'm so happy for you both." Twilight could see Aunt Lucy had used the afternoon well — Jenny was filled in on the whole love story beginning so long ago.

Although tempted to talk until the wee hours, the two sisters wisely suggested bedtime at an early hour in view of the Sunday activities. For this night Jenny would share Twilight's bed. Aunt Lucy had already packed all her clothing except what she would need for the wedding so it would be a simple matter the next day to move Jenny into her room.

"Unless you'd rather have that room?" Jenny questioned. "It's a little larger."

Twilight was positive. "Not at all. I wouldn't trade my own room for anything. I've learned too much there!"

When Jenny's deep, even breathing told Twilight her sister was asleep, Twilight slipped from the big double bed and crept to the window. The moon was shining. It was a beautiful night, and tomorrow was Easter. In spite of the ache in her heart, she was young and full of hope. On a night like this it was hard to regret or fear for the future. With a little smile she stole back to bed and soon slept close to her precious sister, whose life had hung in the balance while she had been gone. Perhaps it was the very shadow of death that had touched Jenny that caused Twilight to move a little closer, pushing back a stray lock of hair from the sleeping girl's brow. In the moonlight Jenny looked like the little girl who used to creep into Twilight's room after a bad dream. With a prayer of thankfulness on her lips, Twilight slept.

When morning came there was excitement enough in Aunt Lucy's house for an army. All three of them chattered throughout their preparations for a big day. Twilight could hardly wait to show off her sister. Jenny was eagerly looking forward to brand-new experiences away from the city where she had lived so long. As for Aunt Lucy! Twilight couldn't believe how helpless she had suddenly grown. It seemed it had finally dawned on her that this was her wedding day. Jenny found her standing on the porch looking into the crisp morning with not even a sweater for warmth. Twilight caught her gazing out the window when she should have been getting ready. So it was with laughter and mingled relief that they finally got themselves to the Golden West Lodge just as the sunrise service was starting.

Never had Twilight seen Lake Chelan look so beautiful. There was a hush over the area, almost a reverence, she thought. Not a ripple marred the glassy image of the water. Again a silent prayer of thankfulness rose within her.

As long as they lived, the sisters would never forget that Easter Sunday. The joy of being together, the love for one another, the beauty of the day, all combined to provide an experience that sank deep into their hearts.

Although a stranger to Stehekin, Jenny was enchanted with everything that went on. Never had she seen such simple, open people, accepting her as Twilight's sister.

And the wedding! Twilight thought of her former plans for a wedding and compared them with the beauty of the one she witnessed that afternoon. It seemed a continuation of the beautiful sermon she had heard that morning. Life, love, service to others. They were all part of the words that joined Aunt Lucy and Jingles, no, Jake, she reminded herself with a smile. From this day on they would be one, working together in their beloved country. Oddly enough, all those miles from Seattle and Jeff, Twilight had never felt closer to him than during Aunt Lucy's wedding.

And then it was over. The new family, with Tommy and Honey beaming, drove toward the ranch, wreathed in smiles. Jingles and Aunt Lucy had decided to have a delayed honeymoon that summer for a few weeks and leave Tommy and Honey with the Wilsons. It would be warmer weather then. For now, it was enough just to be together.

While Twilight watched them prepare to leave a daring thought came to her. She rejected it, then deliberately brought it back to consider. As her aunt got into the car she whispered, "Don't be surprised if I take a run to Seattle this week. It's our school spring vacation, you know. If Jenny is going to stay all summer she will need more clothes than she brought."

"Of course," her aunt agreed promptly, but the twinkle in her eye gave away that she knew exactly what Twilight was up to. "It would be such a good chance to renew, uh, old acquaintances for you, too."

Twilight choked back a laugh and solemnly agreed, "Yes, it would."

"Good luck and God bless you," her aunt called as the girls waved to the new Jacobsen family, then turned away to where Miles was waiting to take them home. They could have come in the jeep, now all fixed up for their use, but Miles had insisted on transporting their "loveliness," as he called the pastel dresses they had chosen for the wedding.

Later that evening Twilight broached her plan to Jenny. Outlining what she meant to do, she soon had Jenny in gales of laughter. Her newly acquired impish grin accented the pixieish beauty that had lurked in the background, held down by unsuspected illness, now out in full force.

"It can't fail," she promised. "I can just see Jeff's face when he opens the door and you say 'I was all wrong, I'm sorry, here I am, what are you going to do about it?' " Again she was hysterical with laughter. "If that doesn't thaw him out, nothing would!"

"It's the only way I know how," Twilight confessed, bravely denying the all-gone feeling in the pit of her stomach. What if he didn't respond? What if he just stood there looking through her like a piece of glass? What if . . . Sternly she pushed aside her fears.

"I don't intend to spend as many years wishing I'd admitted I was all wrong as poor Aunt Lucy did," she told Jenny, who agreed soberly.

"Yes, Aunt Lucy had a happy ending after all that time, but how few ever would in like circumstances!" She was thrilled that Twilight, the cool, calm, almost unapproachable Twilight, had done some changing during that period of separation. She had grown so much more human and understanding. Not that she hadn't always been a wonderful sister, Jenny amended her own thoughts loyally, but she was so much warmer now. More down to earth and willing to admit she was wrong. Jenny smiled secretly. No man could resist this new Twilight, especially one who loved her as Jeff did. For in spite of all that had passed, Jenny was fully convinced Jeff did love Twilight. Under the wall of reserve he had built around his great hurt, the feelings were still there. Twilight's method of approach should explode that wall in a hurry.

Jenny's heart gave a little skip of anticipation! She could hardly wait, first to get back to Seattle, then to get back to Stehekin! Seeing her smile of pure joy, Twilight was again lifted out of her own wonderings by the life in her sister's face.

The next day's trip down Lake Chelan was a far cry from the one Twilight had taken to get to Stehekin so many months ago. Then her heart had been raw and hurt, now it was filled with wild imaginings. Then Jingles had come to her rescue as she stood by the rail brooding over the very sister who was now standing with her enjoying the spring day. There was new appreciation of each other between the girls. It would take Twilight a little time to get used to this new woman-Jenny, yet enough of the little girl still flashed through to make her comfortably at home with her sister after their separation.

Aunt Lucy, as usual, had been right. Both of the girls had profited by the sad experience. Good does come out of bad things, Twilight thought. She thought of it again when they were reunited with the Matthewsons. They were so glad to see both the girls there were tears all around, and Mrs. Matthewson had to drown her joyous tears by furiously kneading down her baking so the fresh loaves Twilight and Jenny loved so well would be ready for dinner. Mr. Matthewson's worn face creased in smiles. Never had his girls, as he called them, looked better. Yet there was a shadow in Twilight's eyes that had not completely disappeared.

"Seen Jeff since you got here?" he inquired casually.

Twilight met the concerned gaze steadily.

"I'm going this evening." She didn't add that she had deliberately chosen the evening hours, early enough to still be "her time of day" because there was strength in knowing the shared moments had been most beautiful then. She needed all the strength she could get for this particular errand!

There was a gorgeous panorama of color over the water as Twilight started out to see Jeff. The heavens above were rosy tinted, reflecting hues of orange, yellow, and banks of purpled clouds until it was hard to distinguish between sky and water. Unconsciously the determined girl squared her shoulders, and felt the peace of the evening as she neared Jeff's home. Lifting her chin, she rang the bell. Again. Again. There was no answer. Disappointment welled up within her. No one was home.

Frantically searching in her purse, she found a pen but nothing to write on. Then, noticing a fluttering white piece of paper stuck in the door, she hastily penned a few words and carefully replaced it so the spring breeze would be unable to snatch it away. Her shoulders drooped as she retraced her steps to the bus stop, but the thought of what she had written cheered her and when she arrived back at the Matthewsons' she could assure them, "He will probably be calling later tonight, or if he had to be out late, first thing in the morning."

Although they sensed her disappointment, they hastily agreed, and settled down to catching up on all her experiences with the one-room school, Aunt Lucy and the wedding, etc., until the clock chimed twelve. Each had subconsciously been waiting for the telephone to ring, but it did not.

"He'll come tomorrow," Mrs. Matthewson told her good husband when the girls had gone up to their old rooms for the night. He wasn't so sure.

"Young feller's got a lot of pride. Maybe he won't. But I hope he does," he added fervently.

But in spite of all their concern, and the fact no one ever left the house during the next few days unless someone else was there to answer the phone, the call didn't come. By the end of the week Twilight was growing thin and pale.

Evidently he didn't care anymore. Deep inside she couldn't even blame Jeff. She hadn't trusted him. Maybe he had found someone who did. The Matthewsons and Jenny's reassurance that he was probably out of town did little to help her, and it was almost a relief when the end of vacation came and she and Jenny were on their way back to Stehekin. The way through had helped her once before; it would again, she told herself. She could see that Jenny, despite her protestations, had begun to unwillingly admit she might be right, that Jeff was too proud to continue caring after all those dreadful months. She had reluctantly disclosed that Jeff had been thinking of taking some out-of-the-way assignment but still steadfastly refused to believe he would ignore Twilight's message.

Neither the concerned Matthewsons, Twilight, nor Jenny could have any way of knowing what had become of the message. Even Jeff himself would have been shocked if he had known what a moment of indifference had done. When he arrived home late from a meeting the night Twilight had been there, he noticed the white fluttering paper stuffed in the door. Glancing casually in the dim light, he saw the announcement of a new restaurant opening soon in the neighborhood, but failed to see the few words written so neatly on the back.

Crumpling the page in his hand, he aimed it toward the fireplace on his way to a well-earned rest, never realizing that the next evening the roaring flames would consume the small message with such a big impact:

I'm sorry — will you forgive me?
Love always,
Twilight

followed by the Matthewsons' telephone number.

Chapter 12

Never had Twilight experienced May as she did this year. April had passed in showers and sunshine, promising better days ahead, but May! A time of wildflowers, bird songs, blue skies, and the greenest green everywhere she looked! The spring rains had washed the earth, leaving emerald acres of trees and grass.

Jenny was enchanted. "How can I stand to leave it and go away?" she asked. "It's so beautiful I wish I could stay here always!"

Twilight looked at her curiously. Jenny was so alive these days, so full of the zest for living. It somehow made Twilight feel old and sad. Despite her own unconscious appreciation of all the beauty surrounding her, the silence that continued between her and Jeff haunted her nights. Her days were too full for anything except school. Ironically, now that Jenny was there with her and that problem solved, for the first time a serious problem had arisen at school to plague her. At first she didn't say anything about it at home, but one evening while they sat on the porch in early twilight Jenny asked her pointblank, "What's happening at school? You used to be so eager to tell me everything that was going on. Now you never mention it."

With a quick rush of words Twilight poured out the story. There was a thief at school. Seeing Jenny's shocked look, she nodded her head firmly. No, she hadn't wanted to believe it either. Yes, she was sure.

"It all started shortly after Easter," she commented, remembering back. "The days were warm and everything was going so well. We started leaving the window open to let in the spring air. Then one day Frank, Jr., waited after school and told me he had hated to say anything but his silver-colored Eversharp was gone. I asked if he had hunted through his desk. He had. It was gone. The students take turns helping me sweep up days and I asked Columbine, who was on duty that week, if she had found it in the trash, but she hadn't. He felt badly about it, his folks had given it for a birthday present and he treasured it, but he didn't want to make a fuss and wouldn't let me ask the class.

"A few days later Honey wore a charming little ring Aunt Lucy had found for her. Just a tiny thing, but bright and pretty. She took it off and left it on her desk when she went out to play. Later that day she missed it. This time there was no keeping it from the class. Honey was in tears. All of the students shook their heads. None of them had seen either the ring or the Eversharp. But the worst of it is," Twilight confided, worried, "it hasn't stopped there. Anything left around that is small enough to be picked up and taken seems to disappear. I'm at my wits' end. I don't know what to do! When I talked to the children they all seemed so innocent. Yet I have to ask myself, which one? Which one? One of them is a thief. But there's no way I can convince myself any of them is."

Jenny was quiet for a long time. She knew how hurt Twilight would be if any of her pupils turned out to be less than perfect. This class was more than just a job to Twilight, she loved each of them. Slowly she spoke.

"Could someone be coming in from outside? You mentioned it started when the weather warmed and you started leaving windows open."

Twilight shook her head decidedly. "No one could approach the school without being seen."

"Wild animals?" Jenny put in hopefully, but again Twilight shook her head.

"There are no wild animals around the school. During the winter we used to see

162

more, but now that spring is here with all the games outside they keep pretty much away. The only thing that could even be remotely classified as an animal is Frank, Jr.'s pet crow Sam, who seems to have an uncanny way of appearing just about at closing time and hitching a ride home on Frank's shoulder!"

Jenny smiled in sympathy at the idea of the crow perched on Frank, Jr.'s shoulder, riding blissfully home after flying to school, but it didn't help solve Twilight's problem.

The very next afternoon was the payoff. Twilight's watchband was loose, so in order to avoid losing it she slipped it in her desk drawer. Before she could close it a loud yell from outdoors brought her to the playfield where Tommy had slipped and cut his knee.

"Get me the first-aid kit," she directed Frank, Jr., who capably rushed in, grabbed the kit, then deftly helped her clean and bandage Tommy's knee. By the time the excitement was over and they got back in class it was almost the end of the day. Seeing the open desk drawer, Twilight reached for her watch to slip into her purse, but it was gone! This was far more serious than a missing pencil or ring. It was an expensive watch, a gift from Jeff when she graduated.

"Has anyone seen my watch?" she asked, but every head shook no. Turning to Frank,

Jr., she asked, "Frank, when you came in for the first-aid kit, was anyone here?"

"Just Sam," came the troubled answer. Seeing the doubt in her eyes he said quietly, "I didn't take your watch, Miss Twilight."

Her class had long since discovered her real name, and while the little ones continued to call her Miss Angel, the older ones had adopted "Miss Twilight."

"I know you didn't," she answered him just as quickly. "Even if you had wanted to, which you didn't, there wasn't time enough between your rushing in for the first-aid kit at the back of the room to have gone up front, taken the watch, and hurried back to help Tommy." Gratitude filled the boy's eyes, but before he could reply little Pixie Jones stood straight up in her seat, eyes wide, finger pointing.

"Look! Look at Sam!"

They all swung to where Sam, the pet crow, was preening himself in the sunny doorway waiting for his master. The bright sunshine caught something sparkling, something tiny, and reflected it into the classroom. Catching his pet, Frank, Jr. removed the sparkling object. It was a bead.

"It's from my bead necklace," Pixie shouted, "the one I lost last week!" It was indeed. The tiny bead had been caught in Sam's feathers.

Twilight was weak with relief, but disgust shone in Frank, Jr.'s eyes.

"I knew crows took things but who would have thought Sam was a thief!" He glared at the bird. "What did you do, come in when we were all outside?"

As if to show his complete indifference to Frank, Sam flew across the room, snatched up Twilight's pen, and started out the door.

"Follow him," she shouted, and with one accord the entire class trailed after the crow, stumbling over each other in their efforts not to lose him. Luckily the nest he had built wasn't too far from school and he lighted in the top of a tall fir tree. Miles Cummings, who had dropped by to pick up Mike and joined in the chase, was laughing helplessly as the older boys climbed the tree and over the protests of the chattering crow stripped the nest of everything that was missing — and then some! There lay Frank Jr.'s Eversharp, Honey's ring, Twilight's pen, Pixie's bracelet, the list went on and on. There were shiny marbles, two pocket knives that had been gone for a long time, and pencils by the dozen.

"What a looter!" Columbine exclaimed, reaching in and taking the dirty red ribbon that had once spotlessly held back her hair. "But I'm glad it was you, Sam, you don't know any better, you're only a crow."

From the looks in the faces around her Twilight could see a reflection of Columbine's words. None of them would have been able to bear the thought that one of them was dishonest. As for Twilight, she was so happy she felt like bursting.

"Class dismissed!" she managed to say weakly, and everyone cheered. She walked over to Sam, now indignantly perched on Frank, Jr.'s shoulder, chattering away.

"As for you, young man, you either learn how to act at school or don't come visit any more." The mock dignity in her voice had them all laughing together and lightened the tension.

When they had gone she walked slowly back to school with Miles. Mike had teased his father to let him go home with Frank, Jr., so Miles would drive Twilight home. It was a lovely walk, spring air filled with relief at having caught the unrepentant thief, but Miles saw the shadow that had filled Twilight's eyes since her trip to Seattle.

"Want to talk about it?" He held out a friendly hand to help her over a fallen log they had all somehow ignored in the mad chase after the crow. For a moment she resisted his kindly concern, then faced him squarely. This was Miles, her friend, someone who cared about her but asked nothing except friendship such as he gave. She could trust him. She hadn't been able to bring herself to talk too much about Jeff with Jenny. She was afraid Jenny would still harbor traces of feeling she had been to blame if she knew how Twilight felt.

Miles dusted off a spot on the board porch and they sat down in the warm sun. Twilight found herself telling him the whole story. How she had found Jenny in Jeff's arms. How she had fled, leaving no word, assuming the protective "Miss Angel" identification. How she had fought bitterness, but throughout the long winter at Stehekin had come out on top, determined to harbor no resentment no matter what came.

"I was so glad to see Jenny here, unannounced," she told Miles happily. "For a long time afterward I blamed myself for not being there while she had to go through surgery. But Aunt Lucy and Jenny showed me it had been for the best. You know Jenny as she now is, a woman. Before last fall she was a girl, dependent on me for everything."

Miles shook his head disbelievingly. It was hard to picture Jennet Trevor as anything other than what she was now, self-sufficient and confident.

Twilight went on. "I've grown, too. I realize now how my rushing off must have appeared

167

to Jeff, the act of a silly, irresponsible child. But there's nothing I can do to erase that memory."

"Why don't you tell him?" Miles suggested gently.

Twilight's narrative faltered, but she raised her chin in the expression he had learned to know so well.

"I tried. I really tried." Her words were almost a sob.

"When we went to Seattle for Jenny's clothes I went to his home." She described leaving the note when he wasn't there, then the hours and days of waiting for a response — which didn't come.

Miles shook his head in silent sympathy. He could see how much she cared, and yet —

"Twilight, even though he didn't respond it doesn't mean he has forgotten you. I know how I would have felt if I had been Jeff. From what you tell me, his love was much the way I felt for Mike's mother. If she hadn't trusted me —" The words fell off into stillness.

A pang of fear clutched Twilight's heart. "Yes?"

"It would have taken me time to forgive. You were here, busy with your new world of teaching, and of beauty. Away from all you knew. Jeff was left there among all your friends, having to admit he didn't know where you were. Worried about Jenny. Wondering where you had gone. Torn, and bitter. It will take time, Twilight. Give him time."

The reasonableness of Miles's words got through to Twilight. She nodded in agreement.

"But what if he has forgotten me?" Her tone was desolate.

"If he is the kind of man who could so easily forget, then is he really the kind of man you want to spend your life with?" The question was earnest.

Twilight remembered Miles's words so many weeks ago about how he was interested in no other woman except as a friend. That was the way she had thought Jeff would be. True, no matter what. If, as Miles had pointed out, he could so easily find solace elsewhere, was he what she wanted? Her parents had been such a monument to what marriage could be that Twilight wanted no less for herself. Now she faced the question honestly and finally said, "No, Miles, he isn't." Fearing the solemnness of the moment she jumped up and laughed.

"Now that we have solved the problems of the world, nation, and state, how about helping me hang some pictures? The students have been doing pressed wildflowers with watercolor painting and it is a little beyond my reach without someone to steady the chair."

Admiration shone in Miles's eyes. She was a winner! But he only replied, "Reckon so."

He was amazed at the quality of some of the pictures. "Hey, these are really good." The pupils had done a beautiful job in finding and pressing the flowers. Even those of the youngest were pretty, but simple. Twilight stepped up on a stool she sometimes used for reaching higher areas and smiled smugly down at him.

"Of course. We don't turn out any but quality work in this shop, sir."

Catching her mood of gravity changed to humor, he disdainfully replied, "What about this one?" pointing to a big paper where the children had cleaned their brushes. "Modern art?"

"Goon!" In her laughter she rocked the stool and came down with a crash, nearly falling. Miles caught her just before she tipped over and with his arm around her helped straighten her uncertain perch.

In their noise and laughter neither had heard the sound of a car approaching. Neither saw the handsome, gray-eyed, dark-haired stranger who hesitantly stepped through the door left open to the spring air. For a moment his eyes rested on the beautiful girl in Miles's arms, heard the sound of her joyous laughter, and something within him leaped to life. But a moment later a curtain dropped over his face, leaving it masklike and lifeless. The sound of his voice pierced their mirth.

"Miss . . . Miss Angel, I believe it is? Your sister asked me to kindly stop by and give you a lift home." There was challenge in the look he shot at Miles, and Twilight straightened up horrified. Clutching at Miles for support, she licked dry lips nervously, the first joy of seeing him crushed by the look of scorn on his face.

Then she managed to whisper nervously, "Miles, I'd like you to meet . . ." but before she could complete the sentence the stranger had gone, leaving the doorway empty and still and her last words fluttering away to nothing . . .

"Meet . . . Jefferson Stone."

Chapter 13

Miles stared at Twilight unbelievingly. "Impossible!" he rejected the idea, but Twilight's frightened eyes convinced him. An ironic smile crossed his face as he said, his lips twisting,

"Jefferson Stone! So that's who he is!"

Now it was Twilight's turn to stare, bewildered. "What do you mean, that's who he is? I told you about Jeff."

"Yes, you told me about Jeff, but I didn't connect it with the name Jefferson Stone." Watching her anxiously, Miles dropped his verbal bomb.

"Jefferson Stone is the new man on the staff of the National Park Service here . . . I will be his boss."

Twilight gasped. "You mean . . . ?"

"Yes." The decided shake of Miles's head left no room for doubt. "We need another forester on the staff. His application was far beyond the others in quality, so he was selected. I even made a special trip to interview him and decided he was just the man for the job."

Twilight was thunderstruck. "But how . . . he didn't know I was here, he couldn't have!"

Miles nodded. "I'm sure he didn't. I imagine he is still a little worried about Jenny's health and wanted to be close enough to check on her if she decided to spend the summer here. This is an opening for summer, with the possibility of year-round employment if he is interested after summer ends."

Twilight couldn't seem to recover her senses. How she had longed to see Jeff and clear up their misunderstanding. My misunderstanding, she corrected silently. Now he was here in the land she loved, but further away than ever. The look on his face as he had refused to acknowledge former acquaintance still pierced her to the quick.

"How could he believe anything so silly!" she demanded of Miles, who was still observing her cautiously.

He grinned wryly, lifting one eyebrow. "The same way you did."

In a flash she saw the situation from Jeff's point of view. She had been unjust in her feelings, disappeared. Months later in a remote area he finds her in some other man's arms. What else could he think?

Twilight drooped suddenly like the tiny flowers now wilted on her desk. Tears filled her eyes, making them look like drenched pansies in a summer rainstorm. Disappointment sat on her shoulders like a mantle. Now things would never be straightened out!

Miles noted the droop to the beautiful lips, the shadows beneath the great purple eyes.

"There's one thing about it, Twilight," he said quietly, and something in his voice lifted her gloom just a little. "From your friend's reaction, it is obvious he still cares for you. If he didn't, your falling into my arms at the most inopportune moment wouldn't have bothered him in the least."

Remembering the glacial stare Miles was evidently choosing to ignore, Twilight shook her head wearily.

"I think I'd like to go home now."

In silent sympathy Miles drove her to the little cottage. There was nothing more he could say.

"Don't forget drama practice tonight," he called as she slowly walked up the path, his keen eyes seeing the intent way she had glanced around to make sure no other car was there.

Twilight nodded indifferently. The little skit they were working on for an end-of-the-school-year program paled into nothingness compared to the latest shattering blow. As he drove off, she took a long breath, braced herself, and opened the door. Jenny's good cooking assailed her, the hominess of the little house greeted her tired nerves. Jenny had taken to housekeeping like a duck to water. She spent hours with Aunt Lucy ferreting out new recipes and Twilight was the willing guinea pig for what Jenny called her "messes," most of which turned out surprisingly well.

"Did Jeff find you?" The sparkling smile died on Jenny's lips as she stood between kitchen and living room, spoon in hand.

"He found me." Twilight's voice was flat.

Quick to catch the desolate note in her beloved sister's voice, Jenny said practically, "Well, let's eat first, they you can tell me about it. Twilight time is always a good secret sharing time of day."

In spite of the delicious dinner, Twilight could scarcely swallow a mouthful, and as soon as dishes were done and the kitchen cleaned up she said impulsively, "I can't wait until twilight, Jenny. Besides, we have that drama practice tonight. Let's go for a walk and get back before Miles picks us up."

It was a beautiful evening as they wandered through the trees behind their little home. Filling her lungs with good clean air, Jenny commented laughingly, "Have to fill them up for all the time I'll spend in the city!" but she sobered when there was no response from her sister.

Dropping down on a fallen log she demanded, "All right, what happened? When Jeff appeared at the doorway today with that big grin of his, I was delighted. What better place for a reconciliation than all this?" She waved at the quiet scene before them. Sleepy birds now starting to quiet for the evening. Flowers nodding on tired heads. Peaceful, silent, healing.

"I almost blurted out that I was with you when he approvingly asked how I'd happened to get to live here. I told him it was Aunt Lucy's place, and that she was married now. I even told him all about Jingles and all the friends I'd made here."

She paused for a moment, then confessed, "Some imp of mischief got into me then and I decided that instead of telling him my room-mate was you, I'd let you tell him yourself! So I merely said that I had a wonderful girl living with me here and her name was Miss Angel and she taught the one-room school. Would he mind stopping by and picking her up?"

Twilight took up the story. "He did just that. But 'Miss Angel,' who turned out to be his ex-fiancee, was clutching frantically at Miles Cummings, who had saved her from a bad fall off a high stool."

"Oh, no!" Jenny's eyes rounded with horror. "What did he do?"

Twilight mimicked Jeff's voice in a tone Jenny could not mistake. " 'Miss . . . Miss Angel, I believe it is? Your sister asked me to kindly stop by and give you a lift home.' Then he marched out the door like a soldier with flags waving, head erect, shoulders set in a way that would stand for no argument."

Jenny's sympathetic nature was touched by Twilight's pathetic attempt at humor. Quick tears sprang to her brown eyes.

"It's all my fault," she said tonelessly, all the fun gone from the slender frame. "Why didn't I just tell him you were here and would be glad to see him?"

"It wouldn't have mattered." Twilight was sure on that point. "When he saw me in Miles's arms, nothing could have convinced him that I was innocent."

"Oh, dear!" Jenny was aghast. What could she do or say to help Twilight? "Do you suppose I should talk to him?"

"With him," Twilight automatically corrected her sister's grammar, then burst into laughter mingled with tears at her own comment. Jenny let her cry. It was the best medicine she could think of. After a time Twilight mopped up her face ruefully and stood up, brushing bits of leaves and dead grass from her skirt.

"We'd better get back to the cabin," she reminded. "We barely have time to get cleaned up for tonight's rehearsal." Then with a bitter twist of her lips, she added, "The show must go on."

The next few days were an echo of the little quiet time in the forest. The show must go on. Days to be gotten through somehow. Nights of remembering, blaming, repenting. Even the students saw the change in Twilight.

"You're like you used to be last fall," Tommy told her worriedly.

She looked at him in astonishment. "What do you mean?"

"Kind of like you aren't alive." His pointed remark brought Twilight back to herself. She mustn't let personal feelings interfere with those all-important last days of school. Now that tests were over, with her students passing with flying colors, her last hurdle was the visit from a representative of the Washington State Office of Education. A keenly observant man was coming to note how things were going in the little school. Twilight had merely told the students they would have a visitor and recitations would go on as usual, but she was keyed to a nervous pitch. She didn't want the pupils to be upset and unnatural in their responses, but she wished to heaven she knew just which day Mr. Smith-Jones would come. To Jenny she confessed, "Smith-Jones! I can just see him, dour, spectacled, peering down a long nose, criticizing everything we're doing. Well, as the proverb goes, 'this too shall pass.' "

In spite of her sister's light tone, Jenny knew how concerned Twilight was. Not only would the results of the visit go into her personnel file at the university, it would be considered in relation to just how valid the little Stehekin school was, also. Day after day passed and still he did not come, and then one morning a stranger appeared in the doorway. Not the scholar of Twilight's imaginings, but a well-dressed man of middle age. Naturally serious, yet Mr. Smith-Jones was totally observant. He joined in the children's play at recess and sat quietly in the back of the room during classes. At the end of the day he thanked Twilight for her hospitality.

Something in his look gave Twilight courage to extend the invitation she had pondered over all that day. Hesitatingly she asked, "As long as you are staying over this evening to catch the ferry back tomorrow, perhaps you would be interested in our little program tonight." She went on to explain how the community had appreciated the Thanksgiving and Christmas programs so much the children had teased for "just one more" before school was dismissed for the summer.

Mr. Smith-Jones's eyes sparkled. "I'd love it!" he exclaimed. "In fact, I may even stay over an extra day and see something of the area surrounding and talk with the School Board members." His warm approval eased the tension in Twilight. She knew the School Board members would have nothing but good to say of her work. Now she wanted to give Mr. Smith-Jones a little background on the particular program he would see.

"It's hard to express exactly why I chose what we were to do," she began diffidently, but his manner soon had her chattering away.

"These students live in an almost totally different world than many city children. When they leave the one-room school for higher education, they are also leaving family ties and warm friendships at quite an early age. They are faced with a new way of life." She was silent for a moment, then finished with a little rush of words.

"I have really learned to care for these youngsters, although Frank, Jr., Columbine, and Mike are certainly too old to be called youngsters! Anyway, they will be leaving at the end of this school year. I talked it over with Aunt Lucy and she helped me come up with a little drama that should be fun, but also informational."

She broke off with a laugh. "I'm not telling any more. It would spoil it. But I think you may enjoy tonight's performance."

Mr. Smith-Jones smiled. "I think so too. I'm also looking forward to meeting your Aunt Lucy. I've heard good things of her work."

Mr. Smith-Jones was not disappointed in the evening. Neither were the parents and friends who crowded the little school. Even Jefferson Stone slipped in unnoticed by anyone except Jenny, taking an out-of-the-way position in the back. It was just as well for Twilight that she didn't know he was there. Frankly, Jeff was curious. It was hard to relate the sophisticated Twilight he had known with the glowing reports of the "Miss Angel" he heard on every hand. Only Twilight herself, Aunt Lucy, Jenny, and Miles knew of their former relationship, so the friendly country folks were free to sing her praises loud and long. Tonight he wanted to see for himself just what she had done with the unusual teaching assignment.

By popular demand Mike Cummings had been selected to act as Master of Ceremonies/ Narrator for the play. He had painstakingly written out the entire script on long parchment paper, rolling it around two branches to resemble a scroll. His Court Jester costume concocted by Aunt Lucy and Mrs. Wilson was a masterpiece of its kind. Its jaunty red cocked hat set off the mischievous grin beneath the feather adorning it. "Ladies and Gentlemen! Tonight we bring to you an original, unpublished, premiere performance of a play. Written by Miss Twilight Angel [the children had voted on the name beforehand], it incorporates lighting, costumes, hard work, and pantomime. I give you" — with a dramatic flourish of his hand to the curtained off area — "Idle Hour Idols."

Never had an audience sat more entranced, most of all, Jefferson Stone. He hadn't realized Twilight's talent for writing. She had taken commonplace terms and turned them into a real message. Mr. Smith-Jones laughed until the tears came. The parents proudly watched each performer, motionless as the old game statues which left each perfectly still, light trained on them. It was even hard to distinguish who was who underneath the carefully prepared costumes.

Mike's narration flowed easily. He was in his element, doing what he loved, as the procession of characters crossed the stage.

"Today is a gloriously enlightened age. But have we put away our idle hour idols? No!"

He proved his point with living examples.

"Father Time." An old man, white-haired, wobbly beard. Was that Frank, Jr. beneath the bent form hobbling across the stage and freezing in place? "He is a thief. He robs people of their most precious asset . . . fleeting moments, happy hours, sunlit days. He leaves sadness that time could be gone so quickly."

Pixie Jones as Lady Luck. Gauzy draperies floating. Delicate, fragile, beckoning "follow me." Untrustworthy, yet precious in the eyes of those worshipping at her altar.

"The Grim Reaper." Mike's voice deepened to hoarseness as the black-shrouded figure poised crouched during his narration. "Blamed. Feared. Dreaded. Yet often more merciful than given credit for."

Dame Rumor and her twin brother Public Opinion nearly brought down the house. The court plaster on the huge plastic noses tended to slip as Mike pointed out how they found the chink in each one's life, ruined lives, broke friendships, and stole peace of mind. Yet how many bowed before them, not from love, but from fear.

The procession continued, each child having a part, each doing a beautiful job. Not a hitch in the little drama unfolding before them. Guardian Angel, known for good and evil, praised or blamed for every trophy or sin imaginable. Golden Opportunity, beckoning like Lady Luck had done. Last Chance. Many others. Mike's voice continued with his narration, humorous or serious as the figure demanded. At last the small space filled with characters, then there was a pause. Each sat silently, expectantly, waiting for the finale. The lights dimmed, the little figures seemed to melt into obscurity, then across the area floated a figure in white.

Never had Columbine been more beautiful than at that moment. When she gracefully reached the front of the lighted area, a blue spot was turned on her. Proudly she stood, a flashlight masked to look like a torch in one hand, a Bible in the other.

Mike's voice was reverent. Even he had not seen Columbine in her final costume and lighting. In a voice low, but clearly audible to each one in the room he announced, "There is one idol that deserves to be kept in our hearts, and only one. She stands pure, untouched by the efforts of men through the ages to down her. She has been burned at the stake, persecuted, tortured. Still she shines throughout our lives. For she is Truth." Softly at first, then growing more audible was the magnificent though untrained voice of Jingles.

"God Bless America, land that I love."

Jenny's voice was the first to join his. Then Miles's. Then the Wilsons', and the Richards', and the Joneses', and all the others. The school year was nearly ended. The little program was over. But before other lights could be turned on, a set-faced man rose from the back and slipped away into the night. He had seen the look of fondness passing between Twilight and Miles at the successful completion of the little play. He had seen and read into it far more than existed.

Now he wrestled with his own feelings as he blindly drove to his assigned cabin. He thought again of the impact the simple drama presented by children had had on all who were present, himself most of all. And he groaned to himself as he sped away from the one-room school.

This, this was the real Twilight. Far greater than he had ever known. More completely a person than he could ever have dreamed. If he had loved her in Seattle, he worshipped her here in the setting that seemed almost created for her. The talent, the beauty, the caring that showed in her work. All had been his . . . and now she was lost. Lost to him forever, and ironically, claimed by the man who was his supervisor in this job he had chosen to get away from his own memories of Twilight!

"I'll go away," he told himself, but was

struck with remembrance. When he had accepted the job, he signed a contract to stay for the summer at least. It wasn't in his code to break his word. But could he stand three months here in this land, beautiful as it was, working for the very man who would one day claim Twilight?

Chapter 14

Last day of school! Twilight's anticipation was mingled with regret. This first year of teaching had meant so much to her she hated to see it end. She had steadfastly refused to face the future. It was enough to finish the school year first. Deep inside she knew that if she wanted to get a job back in Seattle and be with Jenny she had better get her credentials updated. Yet the flicker of hope within refused to die. How could she leave Stehekin with Jeff there, even though he continued to ignore their relationship?

Still, it was with a light heart that she packed a big hamper for the last-day-of-school picnic. Several of the parents who were free were coming in to join the festivities. There were games and races planned for each age in school, and prepared so that hopefully each student could win some kind of prize. Twilight was tender-hearted and wise enough to realize how important it was that each child be praised for something, no matter how little it was. For the three eighth graders who would be leaving she had purchased token gifts. Aunt Lucy had assured her it would be all right, and after much thought, she had selected pen and pencil sets for each, wrapping them carefully, tying the boys' packages with red ribbon, Columbine's with yellow.

All morning there was murmured excitement and it was well that Miss Angel had prepared a different type of schedule. A spelling match among the older ones, followed by a simpler one for the little ones. Arithmetic races on the board. True to Twilight's expectations, each student had been able to win a prize for some type of schoolwork. Honey Jacobsen was so proud of the big blue hair bow she had won in spelling she nearly burst, while the Jones children walked off with honors in spelling, and the Richards twins swept the field in arithmetic. The older children, Mike, Frank, Jr., and Columbine, and Tommy, excelled in the sports events, and little Tara Wilson stood entranced in front of the miniature watercolor she had won in the potato race.

It was a happy bunch of children who filled their plates at the long table of food that had been set up. The ladies surrounded their offerings, comparing recipes, thoroughly enjoying themselves. It was Honey who first asked the question uppermost in everyone's minds.

"Miss Angel, will you be my teacher next year?" Twilight didn't know what to say. Part of her shouted a loud "yes!" while another part held back. Her place was with Jenny — or was it? Jenny had come into her own at Stehekin. Perhaps even more than Twilight she had found her way through. She was a woman, capable of managing her own life, closer to Twilight than ever before, but less dependent. Then too there was Jeff.

Fortunately before the silence following Honey's question became uncomfortable a distraction saved her the necessity of answering. As usual it was Tommy who had fallen, cut knee demanding a Band-aid. In the general confusion the question remained unanswered except in Twilight's own heart.

And then it was over. The food was packed away. The students, one by one, had brought their beloved teacher some little remembrance. Columbine, Rusty, and Pixie had chosen salt and pepper shakers in the form of tiny squirrels with quizzical expressions on their faces. Tommy and Honey offered a box of spicy cookies Aunt Lucy had baked that morning, packed in a beautiful little wooden box that Jingles had made one winter. Tara, lover of beauty, and her big brother Frank brought a curiously carved pin for her dress. The Richards twins gave hankies, embroidered with awkward stitches, obviously their own work. But the biggest surprise was from Mike Cummings. It was a beautiful book all about the North Cascades with pictures of Stehekin included.

Twilight's eyes were filled with tears at their thoughtfulness.

"I'll never forget any of you," she promised. Something in her voice kept them from asking again if she would be back in the fall. Instead they told her how they would come to the cottage and go berry picking. With final good-byes, they were gone. Only she and Jenny were left to sweep the floor for the last time and lock the schoolhouse. Jingles would see to its final closing later.

Jenny looked back thoughtfully as Twilight walked ahead, refusing to take one more look at the little log building where she had both taught and learned so much. Her sensitive nature saw how deeply Twilight felt about this day. To her it must appear to be the end. Jenny secretly hoped it was but a beginning, but she wisely kept still. She had wanted to go to Jeff pointblank, but Twilight wouldn't hear of it.

"I wrote and apologized, yet he refused to even recognize me," she maintained bitterly.

"It's evidently the way he wants it." Then she said no more.

Hurrying to catch up with her sister, Jenny called out, "Twilight, let's take a holiday! We haven't been able to see everything there is to see. Let's get into some old clothes and go hiking." Her bright voice pierced the depression beginning to settle over Twilight and her eyes shone.

"Let's!" In a matter of minutes they were scrambling toward home and less than an hour later they set off. Even in late May the afternoons and early evenings were cool. The mountains brought twilight early to their little home so Twilight insisted they take heavy cardigans, even though the day was sunny.

"We aren't planning to stay out overnight," Jenny objected, but Twilight was adamant.

"It gets cold up here!" She caught up the light rifle Tommy had taught her to use.

"You're not carrying that!" Jenny gasped.

Twilight hesitated, then looked her sister square in the eyes. "Little sis, you don't know all about this country." She laughed at her schoolteacherish tone.

"Neither do I, for that matter," she confessed. "Jingles made me promise to take it anytime I went away from the cabin."

"Even for just a walk?"

"Even for just a walk. He said you just

never could tell when you'd need it. It isn't all that heavy, and this is a big country."

Jenny said no more but the respect for her sister grew by leaps and bounds. What a girl! If Jeff could only . . . she put aside the thought as the hiking got rougher. Twilight had chosen to strike into an area they hadn't explored before behind their little home. There wasn't much of a trail, but Twilight knew Tommy had told her that one cut across a little way back of their cabin, and soon she called back gleefully, "Here it is! This is the woodsy trail that leads straight across from our place to Jingles's. Why don't we walk over and surprise them? Jingles will give us a ride back later. Besides, Tommy said it's really beautiful in these woods."

Indeed it was. The great trees above dwarfed the girls, and there were moss and needles on the ground, making it a springy carpet beneath their feet. They could catch glimpses of blue sky through the trees, and even Jenny was glad to pull the unwanted sweater close around her shoulders. Suddenly noticing some bright flowers off the path, she darted for them, followed by Twilight, who was vastly amused at Jenny's enjoyment. Her sister was like a little girl again, picking a flower here, darting ahead to gather a large cone, or rock, until the pockets of her sweater sagged toward the ground. While Jenny was occupied with her gathering, Twilight was free to think, and it wasn't until Jenny, rosy face shining, announced, "I guess that's enough. Maybe we'd better go back now," that Twilight came to herself. She had followed Jenny's devious path of collection, little heeding which direction they were headed. Now she stood stock-still, wondering just where they were.

The light overhead had begun to dim, and the trees were so thick she couldn't tell which direction was west. Not wanting to alarm her sister, who was obviously in her seventh heaven out in the woods, she struck off in the direction she thought was toward the dim trail they had been following. She didn't notice Jenny's eyes widen. She had thought the trail was in the other direction. After several minutes of walking Twilight began to get alarmed. Nothing looked familiar. Changing course, she struck off more toward the right, but again nothing looked like anyplace they had been.

By then Jenny had come up abreast of her, flowers drooping in her clenched hand, sagging sweater pockets nearly hitting the ground.

"Are we lost?" Her tone of voice showed Twilight that she was a little scared, but not panicky.

"Not exactly. I'm just not quite sure where we are."

"What's the difference?" Jenny demanded laughingly, but a quick sob suspiciously started in her throat, covered by a cough that fooled neither of the girls.

"Let's try over there. It looks a little lighter." Twilight led the way through the deepening gloom to where the trees seemed a little less dense. Sure enough, it brought them out to a little open space, but Jenny could see by the look on Twilight's face she had never been there before.

Puzzled, the two girls stared at the clearing, then back at the timber.

"We can't find our way back through that timber," Jenny said practically. Twilight nodded. There was a stream ahead. What was it Tommy had taught her? Follow down the stream and eventually you'll come out to the main river? She wished she had been paying more attention, but who would have thought she would ever be in such a predicament?

By now the May twilight was almost gone. It was perfectly clear they wouldn't get any further tonight. Twilight looked at Jenny, whose brown eyes were staring furtively at the dark timber behind her.

"Well, we won't be the first ones to get

caught out overnight! Sure am glad we wore those sweaters, and look!" She reached triumphantly in her pocket, drawing out two very mangled candy bars. "We won't starve, either!"

Jenny's chin came up in Twilight's own motion. Not for worlds would she admit the thought of spending a night in the woods petrified her.

"I wish you smoked," she quavered, trying to be brave.

Twilight stared at her as if she had taken leave of her senses. "What on earth are you talking about?"

"If you smoked you'd have matches and we could build a fire." Jenny's words were so earnest, her eyes so wide, Twilight couldn't help laughing.

"Goon! While you're wishing, why don't you just wish we had a steak and a couple of sleeping bags?"

Jenny's quick giggle heartened Twilight. She didn't want her younger sister to know how frightened she herself was at the prospect facing them. Despite Jenny's good recovery from surgery there was still a protectiveness that Twilight felt. She didn't want anything to set her sister back. Why hadn't they just gone down the main trail, she blamed herself uselessly, then she realized there was no point in even thinking about what they might have done.

"Think of what you can tell your new friends in nurse's training." Twilight struck a supercilious pose.

"Re-ah-lly, my de-ah, you have *no idea!* My sister and I, alone on that mountain! And she was, oh, I hate to say it, but, ah, almost use-less! I, yes, I, was the one who bravely comforted her throughout that long, dark night in the woods!"

Jenny was convulsed with laughter. Twilight's dramatic ability was never more evident than in the imitations she sometimes did, and this one of a haughty girl was excruciatingly funny. Jenny fell to her knees, lifting pleading hands. "Oh . . ." in the tones of an impressed schoolgirl, "tell me more, do!"

"Well" — her sister looked down at her condescendingly — "if *I* hadn't been there, she would have collapsed, I am su-ah, absolutely . . ." Her imitation was broken off midsentence by a horrible scream that brought Jenny into her arms.

"What was that?" Luckily Twilight had been somewhat indoctrinated into woodlore since she had come to Stehekin.

"It's only a screech owl." She pointed to a tree near them where in the dim light they could just barely make out the bundle of feathers that once again emitted the yell that sounded like a woman in pain.

Jenny laughed shakily. "He sure is loud!" She moved away from Twilight, half ashamed at being scared by a bird. Twilight sensed her fear and attempt to overcome it.

"Don't feel badly about being scared," she told Jenny. "Jingles told me he was on the way home one night and one of them screeched in his ear. Quick as a flash he whirled around and shot at it, but only a feather drifted to the ground. He's lived here a long time, but it still can scare a person." Her eyes rounded.

"Hey, wait!" Unslinging the rifle from her shoulder, she released the safety catch and shot into the air, waited, shot again, waited, shot again.

"The distress signal. I almost forgot."

"But will anyone hear it?" Jenny wanted to know. Twilight refused to evade the question.

"I don't know. We'll wait until morning to fire another round. I have a few extra cartridges in my pocket as well as those still left in the rifle."

She laid the rifle aside and beckoned.

"Let's get a drink from the stream and pick out the best place to camp while we still have a few rays of light." Her matter-of-fact tone somewhat restored Jenny to a feeling of normalcy. Quickly they threw themselves down by the small, clean brook and drank their fill. The water was icy, even their teeth hurt.

"Straight down from the glaciers," Twilight explained. In the few remaining moments of daylight they chose the best place to try for a little sleep. A huge stump, hollowed out at the base, would provide some shelter from the night ahead. It was lucky they picked their spot. By the time they had removed the rocks and cones from Jenny's pockets it was pitch black. Pulling their heavy sweaters tightly around them, the two girls huddled together at the base of the big stump. Twilight had thought she couldn't sleep a wink, but neither she nor Jenny had reckoned on how tired they were. By the time the moon rose over the little clearing, the two girls were locked in each other's arms, fast asleep. The day with all its excitement, the long hike, and their fears had worked together for good, and nature's healing sleep overtook them.

With the moon came the advent of the night creatures. Small squirrels and chipmunks stared curiously at the sleeping pair. A tiny rabbit, up long past his usual bedtime, sniffed at them, then hurried to his own burrow. Later that night a doe with her two brand-new fawns came to the stream to drink, not fifty feet away from where the girls lay. The mother raised her head to look at them but sensed no danger to her babies and leisurely moved on after drinking. All night long the moon kept watch over the two lost girls, until in the morning the first ray of sunlight discovered a matching golden glint in Jenny's brown hair, now loosened and tumbled. Like a child playing hide-and-seek, it danced across her to briefly outline her face in its radiance, then it shone deliberately and fully in Twilight's eyes.

Both girls came awake at once, unable for a moment to recall their surroundings. They were cold, and stiff from crouching in the flimsy shelter for the night, and the sunlight felt wonderful. In spite of Twilight's misgivings, Jenny didn't look any the worse for wear and an answering sparkle rose in her own eyes at her sister's smile. Straightening their hair as best they could without a comb, they washed their hands and faces at the stream.

"Look, Jenny!" Twilight pointed out the tracks. "A mother deer and her two fawns were here last night to drink." They could see then that there were other tracks in the soft earth. This must be a regular watering place for the animals.

Never had anything tasted so good as the half a chocolate bar Twilight allowed each of them. Meeting Jenny's questioning look, she told her, "We'll save the rest of it for supper just in case it takes until then to get home."

While her tone was casual, Jenny caught her meaning, and added to her pounding senses, "Or if we don't." Picking up her sweater, now empty of treasures Jenny watched Twilight sling the rifle over her shoulder. They had decided to wait until they walked a little to fire more shots.

Jenny looked regretfully at the little heap of items she had collected — they would only weigh her down if she attempted to carry them. Somehow she knew it might take all the strength she and Twilight possessed to get through that day. It was too early for berries to be ripe, they had no equipment to catch a fish, nothing to cook it with if they did. Whispering a prayer that even at that moment was echoed in Twilight's heart, Jenny silently followed her sister to the faint trail at the edge of the stream and started down the clearing. It could be a long, hard walk. There was no time for fear. Yet even in those moments of recognition of their predicament something within her thrilled to the beauty of the place. Turning for one last look, she saw Twilight's eyes rest on the big stump that had sheltered them for the night.

And then they began their journey.

Chapter 15

It wasn't until the same morning Twilight and Jenny started their long hike down the stream to find help that they were even missed. Miles had dropped by the evening before, but finding no one home, he assumed they were at Aunt Lucy and Jingles's, or one of the other families for the evening. But the next morning when he stopped in again something about the silence struck him as odd. The door was unlocked, but then it usually was left unlocked. He stepped inside and the chill of early morning hit him. Surely they wouldn't have gone without a fire the night before! The cabin was built snugly. Last night's warmth should have been in the air.

Miles noted the absence of dishes in the drainer. He had helped do dishes there enough to know the girls always washed them and left them to air dry after a good hot-water rinsing. His forehead wrinkled. Something was strange here. Obviously the girls hadn't slept there. Shrugging, he went out, but the fact of their being gone was enough to make him drive over to Jingles's before reporting for work. Not wanting to alarm Aunt Lucy, he motioned Jingles aside, never seeing that Tommy, who had been helping mend a piece of harness, edged nearer and heard every word.

"Girls must have decided to stay with someone last night." The statement was really more a question. Jingles shot a lightning-quick look at the concerned Miles.

"Why do you say that?"

"No one home, either last evening or this morning." Miles felt a little foolish as he made the comment, yet a nagging doubt inside was enough to worry him.

Tommy piped up. "They weren't going anywhere! Honey asked Miss Angel and her sister to come home with us, but she said they were tired and were going home. They promised to come over this afternoon."

Jingles straightened up abruptly. "Sure about that, son?"

"Of course." He shook his head emphatically, freckles standing out in the morning sunlight. "Think I'd get something like that mixed up? I ain't a little kid!"

Miles disciplined a laugh. "Of course you're right, Tommy. But they must have changed their minds."

"Nope." Tommy was again emphatic.

"Miss Angel always does what she says she will. Bet they went out for a hike and it got dark all of a sudden. Did you notice if her rifle was there?"

Miles felt like a dummy. Closing his eyes, he visualized the cabin as he had seen it a short time before. Why hadn't he thought to look for that first? He opened his eyes and met Jingles's anxious ones squarely.

"I'm sure it was gone. She always keeps it in the same place. I don't think it was there this morning."

Tommy relaxed visibly. "Aw, she's okay then. I taught her to shoot myself. She'll be all right."

Jingles wasn't so easily satisfied. It was no light matter for two inexperienced city girls to be caught out overnight in this country. If they wandered off in some strange direction it could be days before they found their way to any of the places where help was available. Besides, there were all the dangers of wild country. Ravines, streams to cross, even mother bears with cubs who were especially dangerous. Laying his work aside, he said quietly, "We'd better go find them."

Seeing Tommy's expectant face he added, "You, too, son. Bring Wolf, too. That collie has a good nose."

With all the assurance of experience, he

commanded Miles, "Better go get some of your people, too. It's a big country."

Miles thought of the seriousness in his voice as he rushed back to headquarters to obey. One of those I'll get is Jefferson Stone, he thought. A wave of anger rushed through him. The new man was a whiz at his work, but when he thought of how he had failed to respond to Twilight's apology it burned him to a crisp. Something of his feelings must have shown in his voice as he entered the office.

"Stone. Jeffers. Randolph. Scott. Two women lost in the woods. Get out to Aunt Lucy's cabin immediately. Take some blankets in the rig, apparently they've been out all night. Wait!" He held up his hand.

"Stone, you come with me." He noticed the involuntary tightening of Jeff's knuckles as he added, "It's the Trevor girls."

Jeff was silent until they got in the truck, then inquired, rather sarcastically, "What did they do . . . wander off into the woods?"

"Yes, they did," Miles snapped. "But up here it's no laughing matter. There's a lot of woods, that go on and on. You've been here long enough to see that!"

"Sorry, sir." Jeff dropped behind his wall of reserve again but his seemingly stupid comment had enraged Miles.

"Seems to me you'd be a little more concerned about them, especially Twilight, than that remark indicates!"

Forgetting himself for a moment Jeff shot back, "That's your responsibility now, isn't it . . . sir?" The bitterness in his tone caused Miles's eyes to widen but was like a flash of light illuminating some of his shadowy questions.

Continuing to keep the same pace in driving, he brought his fist down on the dashboard.

"No, it isn't! And the sooner you get it through your thick skull the better!"

A thrill of hope went through Jeff in spite of himself, but he gripped the door of the car and asked, "Are you speaking as my supervisor?"

Miles slammed on the brakes, pulled the car to the side of the road, and faced him squarely.

"No, I'm not! But I'll tell you this, and then I'm done with your moping! I don't care about all the time you searched for Twilight. She made what was the most natural mistake in the world. How would you feel if you saw her in someone else's arms, for example the way you did when she fell off a stool and I caught her to keep her from taking a swan dive onto the floor?" He failed to notice the involuntary start and the gleam that began to fill the steady gray eyes watching him. Once he had started, he decided to give it to him good. All the pity for Twilight and admiration for her filled his voice.

"She came up here torn apart. But she was too big a person to let it make her give up. She faced a new way of life, a challenge in that little one-room school. And yet she never, down deep, stopped believing in you! She told me so herself! And you" — he pointed his finger at Jeff — "you with all your pride! You just couldn't forgive her for not trusting you completely, could you? Yet you've found out how hard it was to trust her in like circumstances.

"What else do you want from her? No, I'm not in love with Twilight. She isn't in love with me either. But I wish she was! I'd make her a life that you and your arrogant unwillingness to forgive will never make! Anyone that could totally reject her the way you've done since you arrived . . . and after she rushed off to Seattle the minute she heard the truth. Rushed off to tell you how wrong she'd been. Of all the time for you to not be home! But even that didn't stop her, she had to leave a note . . ."

The steel grip of Jeff's hand on his wrist would have made a weaker man than Miles cry out in pain. It also served to stop his tirade of bitterness against this man who had caused Twilight so much suffering. Miles continued a little more quietly.

"She had no paper, so she wrote on the back of some kind of ad stuck in your door." Again he was cut off, this time by Jeff's releasing his arm and dropping his head in his hands with a cry of anguish.

"Oh, no! I threw that ad in the fire when I got home late that evening! Will Twilight ever forgive me? All those months, I thought I'd go mad. Searching, questioning, finally facing the fact she never wanted to see me again. Then coming here so unexpectedly and finding her with you . . ." His voice failed.

For a moment Miles stared at the husky man before him. There was no question how much he cared. Then Miles did a strange thing. He smiled, then he chuckled, then he laughed, much as he had done the night so long ago when Twilight had planned to tell him he mustn't get serious about her. Jeff's head shot up, anger in his face, but in the light of such spontaneous mirth he couldn't stay angry. He began to see how they had been at cross purposes with each other when they really only wanted one thing — Twilight's happiness. When he could control his own laughter, he held out his hand silently. Miles gripped it with equal strength, glad at last to have his new employee with him more than just physically. Then he said, "In the meantime, let's get to Aunt Lucy's cabin. Those girls may need us pretty badly."

Jeff conquered the fear rising within him at the thought of what they might find and lifted his chin, swallowing hard. One more thing had to be said before the subject could be dropped between him and Miles.

"I'm sorry . . ." he started, then he shook his head defiantly. "No, I'm not sorry, either! If I hadn't acted like I did you would never have been angry enough to tell me what I needed to know!"

Miles brushed it aside impatiently. "Forget it! I have to have something to spout off about every so often or my men will think I'm getting soft." He met Jeff's grin of understanding, and in that moment a true comradeship was born. He thought to himself, I've always liked this man, that's why I was so disgusted with him for treating Twilight as I thought he had. I didn't want him to be petty and small.

In turn, Jeff's thoughts were following a similar turn. I guess that's why I was so jealous, he thought, admitting the truth to himself. He's such a splendid person I couldn't see how Twilight could help falling in love with him.

Their arrival at the cabin broke their musings and the sight of Jingles, carrying a heavy rifle, Tommy, with his dog Wolf, and several of the other men brought them back to reality.

How ironic, Jeff thought with a twist of his lips. Finally, when I just think I've found Twilight, perhaps I've really lost her . . . this time for keeps. In spite of his newness to the country he respected the ruggedness of the land, yet he kept reminding himself, Stehekin . . . the way through. God help it to be that for Twilight and Jenny. With a start he realized it was the first time he had thought of Jenny. How would she fare? Would it be a setback for her? He hoped not. Quietly he took his place near Tommy and Wolf, who had been given an old shoe of Twilight's to smell.

"Go find Angel," Tommy commanded. Wolf looked at his master, head cocked to one side, then with a final sniff and one loud "woof" started down a little-used path back of the cabin, head up and confident. The men looked at one another and fell into line. There was nothing to go on except Wolf's excellent sense of smell. They might as well all stay together, at least for now. There wasn't much talking. Each man had his own thoughts. Again Jeff's heart cried out for Twilight and Jenny's safety. Since he had come to Stehekin he knew his love for them was far greater than that he had felt the summer before. In the big outdoors love and appreciation of one another weren't crowded aside by the noisy shouts and clamor of the city.

I could be perfectly happy here the rest of my life, he thought in surprise, looking at the blue sky, the clean green forest, the small chipmunks and squirrels. I wonder how Twilight feels about it? Even though she's been a year almost away from civilization itself, would she want to live here permanently? She's a city gal. Could she be happy here? Pushing the thought firmly aside, he followed down the needle-carpeted path. Now was not the time for such dreaming. Enough time for that when she was found, if she could forgive him for all that was past.

A loud barking and a triumphant shout from Tommy up ahead brought Jeff to a little clearing in the trees. He couldn't remember ever having seen a lovelier spot. The stream flowing through, so icy cold and clear. Towering trees against blue, blue sky. Only for a moment was it all imprinted on his consciousness, for his attention was immediately riveted on Tommy, triumphantly holding up a long yarn thread. He was standing near an old hollow stump.

"They slept here," Tommy shouted. "This is from a sweater. And look!" he pointed, exulting. Jeff didn't see anything amazing about the little cluster of small twigs, stones, and dead flowers on the ground, but he caught the significant look between Jingles and Miles.

"Good work, son," Jingles approved, patting the beaming Tommy on the shoulder.

"How'd you ever spot those things?" Jeff marveled.

Jingles cast him a look of scorn. He wasn't too sure he liked this new man. Although Lucy had said nothing of Twilight and Jeff's past association, Jingles sensed they had known each other prior to Stehekin and in his own shrewd way had deduced this man had somehow hurt his "new niece," as he called the girl. So now his answer was short.

"Mister, in this country, you learn to spot anything out of the ordinary. It's a matter of survival. A crushed leaf, a bent branch, any one of those things can sometimes make the difference between life and death." Seeing the stricken look on Jeff's face, he relented and put a kindly hand out to him.

"The girls are all right. See —" He showed Jeff three empty shells he had picked up from the ground. "Evidently they signaled last night. They'll shoot again. Besides, Wolf is pretty keen." Some of the haggard look left Jeff's face and again Jingles was quick to notice. So the young feller cared for Twilight . . . or could it be Jenny? Turning to Tommy, Jingles called,

"Set Wolf on the trail again. They must have a couple, three-hour headstart, but we can catch up. We didn't sleep out last night!" He chuckled. "Those two will be glad for their own beds tonight!" His heartiness seemed to lift the gloom from the little party, and it was with almost light hearts they started on.

Jingles was happy to note the girls had remembered to follow downstream. If they had crossed, or gone up, there was some pretty wild country. But downstream, although it was a long way to any habitation, was fairly easy going. Now if they just didn't run into a bear. Spring, especially this time of spring, could find mother bears and cubs out enjoying the sun, and nothing was more dangerous than an enraged she-bear. Despite his assurance, he for one would be glad to get to those girls. He had come to love both Twilight and Jenny as his own. It would hurt him as much as Aunt Lucy if anything should happen to either of the girls.

Jeff, happily unaware of Jingles's dark thoughts, relaxed enough to enjoy the beauty around him and go back to dreams of the future. Where else could you find country like this? People who cared, who were concerned about each other and their families. Country unspoiled by too many people with their pollution and noise. Scenery almost good enough to digest. What a place to raise children and give them basic values of life that could form a solid rock against later temptations! His face burned at the direction his thoughts were taking, and Miles, noting the red tinge, divined some of what his companion's thoughts must be. He hoped Jeff and Twilight would settle here. What an asset to the little community they would be! Twilight could go on teaching. Perhaps it would come true. His thoughts turned back to his own early days in Stehekin with his beloved companion. There was no sadness in looking back, only the joy of memory.

For perhaps two hours they walked, the sun shining hotter overhead, the men stopping often to drink of the clear, clean stream. Never had Jeff tasted such water. He couldn't get enough of it. Heavy jackets were now tied around the men's waists and each mile seemed to bring them that much closer to the girls.

Of course it would be Tommy, with Wolf far ahead, who was first to spot the prone figure against the tree as they came over a slight rise in the ground. Fear held him motionless, then he flew to the girl's side, only moments before Jeff pounded up, white-faced, to catch Jenny in his strong grasp.

"Jenny! Are you all right?" He almost hated to ask the next question.

Jenny's brown eyes opened, bewildered. Then she burst into tears, clutching Jeff as if she would never let him go, managing to get out, "Oh, Jeff, I'm so glad you came! I've been so afraid! I was so tired I couldn't go on. Twilight said we had to have help. She left me here about an hour ago."

By now the others had gathered around Jenny, who was too exhausted to say any more. One of the men put his coat under her, another covered her feet with his jacket, and Miles brought her a cup of steaming soup from the thermos he had stuck in his pocket. He had to feed her, Jenny was just too tired, mostly from worry over her sister, to help herself, but after a few sips she roused.

"Go find Twilight! Don't you understand? She's all by herself, and hungry, and her ankle is hurt! I couldn't help her, I was too weak!" Crying bitterly, she sank back against the coats, filled with disgust at her own inability to do anything for Twilight.

Jeff was torn between concern for Jenny, who had clearly been overtaxed, and fear of what might befall Twilight. Seeing he could do nothing for Jenny, who after all was only worn out, he and Jingles followed Tommy and Wolf, who were almost out of sight. A commanding shout from Jingles halted them.

"Tommy! Wolf! Wait for us!" Panting with exertion from keeping up with this seasoned mountain man, Jeff pounded to where Jingles was kneeling beside the stream, hands measuring something in the soft mud.

"Bear tracks." Jingles's words were terse. "Mother and two cubs. Let's get going." His very brevity struck a new fear into Jeff's heart.

It seemed hours that they ran, slowed to walk for rest, then ran again in search of Twilight. Her danger now was very real, much more so then merely a night in the woods. Then through the clear air came the sound of shots. Shots from a light rifle, such as Twilight carried. One . . . two . . . three . . . four. Not a distress signal, something far more frightening — the sound of someone shooting for her life.

Chapter 16

The scene facing Jeff as he rounded the bend would be indelibly impressed on his mind, a scene of utter horror. Twilight, scratches on her face, one ankle drawn painfully up underneath her, was crouching high in a huge tree, as near the top as she dared get without straining the swaying branches to a point where they would refuse to hold her slender weight. An even huger bear was halfway up the trunk, spitting and growling in sheer fury, while two round-eyed cubs watched "mama" stalking her prey. Twilight's light rifle had only served to anger the maddened bear further — she was too inexperienced to place a shot where it would have saved her.

For a moment Jeff stood rooted to the spot, frozen, then, casting caution to the winds, he rushed to one of the cubs and caught it up. Squeezing it tightly until it yowled for mercy, he began slowly backing away from the big tree that housed Twilight. Ignoring Twilight's agonized cry of "No, Jeff!" he squeezed the furry cub again and again. Its pitiful wailing did what nothing else could have done, diverted the attention of its mother from Twilight. With a terrible roar she came down the tree trunk with the speed of lighting. Her baleful eyes glared at Jeff, her slow brain taking in this new menace.

"Run!" shrieked Tommy, hopping up and down in his excitement, rifle ready for a shot that wouldn't endanger Twilight or Jeff. But Jeff had other ideas. He didn't want the mother bear shot if he could help it. Holding the struggling bear cub under one arm, he streaked across the clearing to a large group of trees he had noticed. He calculated he had perhaps a minute before the mother bear could reach the ground, and another before she could overtake him. Now his speed and endurance from college track days served him well. Using every ounce of endurance he possessed, he reached the biggest tree and began climbing it, still hanging onto the cub. It was a hard climb, and by the time he reached the sturdy branches above, "mama" was at the foot of his tree. With a desperate prayer that it would hold, he set the cub on the branch next to the trunk, then edged out as near the end as he dared, gave a leap, and clutched a giant branch of a nearby tree. It groaned and cracked under the unexpected weight, but held. Rapidly he performed the same feat once more, by now having put some distance between himself and the large tree where "mama" had reached her lost cub.

In a matter of moments Jeff reached the others, who had rescued Twilight from her perch and helped her back to the edge of the clearing. The second bear cub had watched the proceedings with interest, then with a lonesome look, trotted to the foot of the big tree to peer up through its branches to "mama" and his brother.

"Let's get out of here before he starts howling and brings her down," Jingles ordered. Jeff snatched Twilight in his arms and despite her protests that she could walk, insisted on carrying her until they were well out of sight of the bear family.

"Think I'm taking any chances on losing you again?" he whispered, and if he pressed his lips to her tangled hair, no one noticed but an inquisitive squirrel who had retreated to his home and chattered as they went by. There was no time for explanations. There was no need for them. In those terrible moments of fear the past was erased. Hurt feelings had been eclipsed in the short time period of danger. Twilight smiled wearily. Everything was all right, Jeff was safe. That was the only thing that counted. Jenny would be so glad . . . Jenny!

"Is she all right?" She clutched Jeff's sleeve.

"She's fine, just tired," he reassured her, and Tommy added,

"Yeah, all she needed was something to eat. Looked starved to death!"

But there was nothing starved looking about Jenny when she saw her sister. She jumped from the nest the men had made her and ran as if her life depended on it. Grabbing Twilight, she burst into tears, then laughed.

"What a mess! Do I look that bad?"

Twilight grinned back at her. "Let's just say you wouldn't win any beauty contests right now!"

Jingles insisted on a good long rest before they started back. The men had improvised a stretcher from a blanket and two small saplings nearby and forced Jenny and Twilight to take turns on it. As it turned out, Twilight's ankle wasn't sprained, just badly scratched and sore. She had evidently stumbled over an old log with a stob sticking out. Yet the girls were glad to rest. Even though Jingles knew a shorter way home than the one they had taken, it was a relief to rest part of the time. Jenny's big eyes glowed, shivering with fear, then pride, on hearing how Twilight had climbed the tree and attempted to hold off the bear. Tommy lost nothing in the telling of Jeff's rescue.

"Gramps couldn't get a shot at the bear while she was in the tree, she was too close to Twilight. Then Jeff got her away and there wasn't any need to shoot. Gramps says it's bad to kill animals unless you have to. Besides, those little bear cubs wouldn't want to grow up without a mother."

Something in his tone touched Jenny deeply. "You miss your own mother, don't you?"

A shadow filled the boy's eyes. "Not like I did before Aunt Lucy came," was all he said, but his grimy hand squeezed Jenny's tightly. Ashamed of the moment of emotion he looked at Jeff, walking close to Twilight.

"Is he her fella?"

Jenny smiled. "He sure is!"

"How come he took so long to come up here?" Tommy wanted to know.

"He didn't know she was here."

Tommy eyed her warily, then asked, "How come?"

"They had a quarrel, sort of." Jenny felt it better to leave it like that. "She ran off and came up here. Are you glad?"

"You bet!" There was nothing hesitant in Tommy's grin of approval. He was silent for a little while, then looked at Jeff and Twilight again.

"They gonna get married?"

"I hope so!" Jenny laughed. "They've sure taken their time about it!" She was too happy for her sister to notice the slight frown that crossed Tommy's face, or hear the big sigh that came clear up from his boots. He knew what happened when people got married. They were too busy for anybody else. Oh, not Aunt Lucy and Gramps, they were different, but then they were old, not like Jeff and Miss Angel. His thoughts went back to all the times since Miss Angel came. Now everything would be all spoiled. Jeff would take her somewhere back in the city to live and that would be the end of their good times at school and everywhere. Somehow Miss Angel and Twilight were all mixed up in his mind.

"I liked her better when she was Miss Angel," he muttered, his mood becoming blacker and blacker, his scowl growing until his whole usually sunny face was sour. Deliberately he dropped back to the end of the line, scuffing through the moss. He guessed when he grew up he'd be a hermit. People ruined everything when they fell in love.

If Twilight had known Tommy's thoughts, she would have laughed inwardly. So would Jeff. But totally unconscious of his despair, they laughed and chatted with the others, each holding close the precious thought of being together, even in a crowd of others. There would be time ahead to plan and dream, all the rest of their lives. For now it was enough just to know all the lonely past was over, the end of their tunnel had been reached, and sunlight lay ahead.

It was two tired girls who cleaned up hurriedly and immediately went to bed when they reached the log cabin. Never had it seemed so welcoming! Jingles wanted to take them home to Aunt Lucy, but they demurred. All they wanted was to get some sleep. No wonder — it had been a long, hard two days for them. Jenny was asleep the minute her head touched the pillow, but Twilight lay awake a little longer, savoring the truth that she and Jeff were actually together again! He had managed to slip the ring she had left in the apartment so many months ago on her engagement finger. Tears slipped down her cheeks as she thought of how nearly life could have ended that afternoon. First her own, then Jeff's. After the one cry she had been unable to speak during those short moments when the bear deserted her to go for Jeff. Now the sparkle of the ring seemed to reflect the sunshine coming after the many storms of the past months. A half smile touched her lips, then she too slept.

The sound of giggling finally brought her

out of the dreamless sleep she had fallen into. Jenny stood in the doorway, her own eyelids heavy, but with eyes sparkling.

"Do you realize what time it is?" she demanded as Twilight pushed back her heavy hair and sat up, groaning as sore muscles made themselves known.

"Who cares?"

"I do! I'm starved, and Aunt Lucy has been here." She pointed to the bedside clock.

"Ten o'clock! We slept all afternoon and evening and until ten o'clock!"

"We couldn't have," Twilight denied indignantly, but the hands on the clock disputed her and she couldn't help but laugh. "I'm hungry, too," she admitted sheepishly. "When did Aunt Lucy come?"

Jenny hung her head and moved her bare foot around on the floor. "I don't know, I just woke up a few minutes ago and found a basket and note on the kitchen table. She brought our breakfast. I must have awakened when the jeep left."

Padding to the kitchen, Twilight joined in Jenny's squeal of delight. "Fresh cinnamon buns!"

It didn't take long to pour juice, scramble some eggs, and plow into the basket of buns. In an unbelievably short time the basket was nearly empty.

"How many did you eat?" Jenny questioned, but Twilight only groaned, holding her stomach as mute evidence that she had had her fair share. The sound of footsteps on the porch sent both girls diving for robes to throw over their summer pajamas, then Tommy, Honey, and Wolf bounded in.

"Aunt Lucy went to the store. We promised to stay outside until we heard you," Tommy told them, peering anxiously into the almost empty basket, Honey not far behind.

"There's some left," Jenny reassured them, giving each a bun spread with butter and pouring milk into two tall glasses. They beamed at her but Honey stopped short, bun in midair, and pointed.

"Did that man give you that?" Her eyes met Twilight's accusingly and Tommy turned to stare at Twilight's ring.

"Yes, he did," Twilight answered quietly, but with such pleasure in her face that Tommy lost his appetite. Now he knew for sure Miss Angel would be getting married and going away. Almost afraid to ask, he listened with stopped breath as Honey went right on.

"Are you going to marry that man?"

Jenny cast an anxious look at Twilight. Honey's tone expressed deep displeasure, but Twilight only smiled.

"Yes, I am, Honey." The little girl's next question was harder.

"Tommy said you'd probably go away with him. Do you love him more than you love us? Why don't you stay with us? Who's going to be my teacher?" She began to cry.

Twilight picked up the golden-haired little girl and held her close. How could she explain?

"Remember when Aunt Lucy married Jingles and came to live at your house?" At the little girl's nod she went on.

"She left me here. That doesn't mean she didn't love me any more. But she loved Jingles, too, and so she went to his home."

Up came the head. Blue eyes searched Twilight's face earnestly, but not as closely as those of Tommy, who had listened in silence.

"When I grow up I'm going to marry Tommy," Honey announced in a minute. "Then I won't have to go away from anybody, ever!"

Tommy growled in his throat, red creeping up to his ears.

"You don't marry your own brother!"

But Honey stuck to her guns. "You just wait and see!"

It's a good thing Aunt Lucy chose that moment to return. She had entered a few moments before and heard some of the conversation.

"Maybe she won't have to go away. Jeff told Jingles he loved this country more than anyplace he had ever been." Twilight's heart leaped within her as she looked at Aunt Lucy, not seeing her, but seeing Jeff. What a life it would be! To be able to remain here, with Jeff! Then her face sobered.

"I don't know, Aunt Lucy. He was head of his class, with all kinds of offers. I don't know if he could be happy here permanently or not."

Even the children caught the unhappiness in her voice and wisely remained silent, but as Aunt Lucy bundled them into the jeep, Honey told Tommy, "I don't care. I think it's mean of that man to take our Miss Angel off somewhere else. Don't you?"

Aunt Lucy's sharp ears couldn't help overhearing Tommy's reply through clenched teeth, "Yes, and if he does, he's going to be sorry!"

Chapter 17

Surprisingly enough, Twilight and Jenny liked summer least of all the seasons in Stehekin.

"Don't get me wrong," Twilight told Aunt Lucy, who had come over to spend the day with the girls and help with some sewing for her trousseau, "I love the crisp evenings and the sunny days. But there are so many tourists!"

Aunt Lucy laughed outright. "Don't forget we make our living off those same tourists," she reminded. "If they didn't come, Jingles would have a mighty slim living!"

"I guess that's right," Jenny piped in. "But isn't it lonesome with him gone guiding people into the hills so much?"

"Yes it is," Aunt Lucy admitted. "But it's his job. I knew when I married him it was his way of life. Besides, he loves these mountains, and is never happier than when showing them off to tourists." Jenny caught the quick flash of understanding between Aunt Lucy and Twilight. It was something they shared that she had not yet experienced, the complete willingness to be happy just so long as they were with the men they had chosen. A flash of insight of her own showed that when her time came she would feel the same, and she firmly disciplined the lonely little thought of when she must leave and go back to Seattle for her training, loved though it would be.

Those summer months were beautiful for Twilight and Jeff. It seemed the whole valley shared her happiness and his — with one notable exception, Tommy. It was the worst summer of his life. He had planned to take Miss Angel everywhere, but instead he became so withdrawn and sullen it was hard to recognize in him the happy-go-lucky boy he had been when she came. But in late July something happened that set his world rightside up again. Jenny especially had noticed Tommy's attitude, and at last she went to Twilight.

"I don't want to play tattletale, but I've found out why Tommy is like he is," she said solemnly, looking more than ever like a little girl in her pink-checked slacks and top.

Twilight lay aside her sewing with interest. "For heavens sakes what is it? He's been driving me crazy, and I haven't been able to figure out what's wrong with him."

"He's jealous of Jeff."

The flat answer stopped Twilight short. "He's . . . what?"

"You heard me. He's jealous of Jeff, and all hurt, and afraid you're going away."

Twilight stared at Jenny. "How did you find out?"

Jenny shook her head, but reminded, "You know he was going to show you all the wonderful summer things in Stehekin. Well, you and Jeff are busy evenings and weekends, and Tommy helps at home days so when he's free you're with Jeff. So he's taken me as a substitute and we've become good friends. He's shown me everything! And little by little I can see what he is worrying over."

"But what can I do?" Twilight asked helplessly. "I don't know either what Jeff and my future is going to be. I've wanted to ask but don't quite know how. I thought Jeff would bring it up of his own accord, but he hasn't."

Jenny nodded wisely. "I think you should explain the problem to Jeff. He loves kids and at first Tommy thought the sun rose and set in him. Maybe he would know what to do."

That same evening Jeff and Twilight stepped out the door for their usual walk in "her time of day." Armed with her new knowledge, Twilight waited until they had walked a little way from the house and seated themselves on a log, watching the animal world come to life after the sun had gone down. Often they came to this favorite spot; sometimes they would see a deer, often rabbits, always squirrels. But tonight Twilight had more on her mind than the beautiful evening.

"Jeff —" She hesitated, not knowing quite how to approach the subject. "Have you seen Tommy lately?"

He turned to her in surprise. "Funny you should bring Tommy up, I was just thinking of him. Ran into him at the boat dock with Honey and he barely spoke." He laughed shortly, without humor. "At least he didn't do like Honey. She grabbed Tommy's arm and announced in a stage whisper everyone around heard, 'I don't like that man!' Tommy hushed her and marched off, but the way he looked, I think he agreed!"

Twilight was really troubled now. She told him what Jenny had said that afternoon. Jeff nodded.

"That makes sense. But where did he get the idea you were leaving? Did you tell him I was going to take you away?" There was a curious stillness about him as he waited for her answer but Twilight didn't notice.

She said, "I guess I did say that wives went to their husbands' homes when they got married."

Jeff was quiet for a long time. "Is that what you want, Twilight? To go back to the home in Seattle?"

Twilight didn't know what to say. With all her heart she wanted to shout, "No!" but the way he had phrased the question left her wondering if that was what he himself wanted. It was one thing to fall in love with a country in spring and summer, quite another to live there year round.

She countered with his own question. "Is it what you want?"

"I asked you first," he reminded.

Drawing a deep breath she said, "It's beautiful here . . ." Her voice trailed off.

"But is it what you really want?" Jeff's voice was stern, insisting on complete honesty.

"I'll be happy wherever you choose," she said simply. "But I love Stehekin in a special way. It healed me, it showed me the way through. No other place will ever be in my heart as this is."

"Thank God!" he spoke fervently, startling her with his emotion. "From the time I came here, even when we were miles apart in spirit, I loved this place. I have an opportunity to become a first-class assistant to Miles and you could teach or not as you chose."

For the first time doubt crept in. "I don't know about that, Jeff. Nothing has been said.

The School Board haven't asked me if I would be interested . . ." Again her voice trailed off.

"That's my fault," he confessed. Drawing a crumpled teaching contract from his pocket, he told her, "I've carried it around for a month. Jingles was so sure you'd sign it he gave it to me to give you with the condition that I make sure you wanted to live here before I did."

"You . . . you . . ." Words failed her. When she did get her breath she accused, "All this time! And here I was worrying myself to death, and Tommy and Honey and . . ." She ran out of words and just sputtered.

For a moment Jeff let her rave, then he put in neatly, "Oh, I told him you'd sign it, just wanted to hear you choose for yourself where your home with me was going to be." He leaned forward, eyes gleaming, to drop a kiss on her startled lips, then pulled her close, looking down into the beautiful purple eyes.

"Did anyone ever tell you how lucky this guy is?" His voice was husky, as was hers in reply.

"Me, too!" For a long time they were silent, just enjoying the beauty surrounding them, then with a sigh he stood and pulled her up to her feet.

"I have to work tomorrow — and I have a

feeling when I get through there's a visit to a certain freckle-faced boy that had better be made."

True to his word, the next evening Jeff drove out to the Jacobsen place. He found Tommy hunched up under a tree, staring disconsolately off into space. There was something pitiful about this sturdy youngster who could shoot a bear yet be so lost and lonely at times.

"Hi, there," Jeff hailed, and dropped down on the ground before Tommy could get up. He got right to the point.

"I never did get to thank you for taking care of Twilight for me."

Tommy turned red as a beet. " 'Twasn't nothin'." He turned his head resentfully away from Jeff's broad grin, but the man refused to be put off.

Sizing up Tommy thoroughly, well pleased with what he saw, he spoke firmly. "She's going to be needing some more help pretty soon. You know we're getting married . . ."

"Yeah." The brief syllable spoke volumes.

"Well, I'm going to be busy working and I know she'll be needing some new cupboards and stuff in Aunt Lucy's cabin. I was wondering if you'd be able to help us, like evenings and Saturdays and —"

"Aunt Lucy's?" The hostile look began to

give way to wonder. "You're getting Aunt Lucy's?"

"Sure are. She didn't really want to sell but we don't have much time to get a home ready before school starts . . ."

Tommy looked at him for a moment then barely whispered, "School? Miss Angel's gonna teach school . . . here?"

"Why, of course." Jeff managed to quell the laugh inside and look surprised. "That is, unless you don't want her."

"Don't want her?" The look Jeff got was pure scorn, but it melted before the continued friendly steady gaze between man and boy.

"I thought you were going away." The words spoke volumes.

"Where'd you get that dumb idea? We're staying." For a moment Tommy just stared, then he let out a warwhoop that brought Honey running. When she saw who was with Tommy she stopped short, mouth open.

"I don't like . . ." she began, but Tommy shouted at her,

"Honey, they're going to stay. In Aunt Lucy's cabin. And Miss Angel is going to be our teacher again!" Honey was all smiles at this news. She shyly slid up to Jeff and put her hand in his.

"I like you, Jeff," she told him.

"I like you too," he solemnly replied to

Tommy's delight, then he shook hands with each of them, making a pact of friendship right then and there.

Aunt Lucy had observed the byplay from a short distance away and as usual had the last word.

"My stars! If I'd known you had any such idea in your mind, Tommy . . ."

But Jeff smoothly put in before Tommy's embarrassment turned him any redder, "Tom's going to help me do some building if you don't mind."

Aunt Lucy's eyes twinkled and she saw through his ruse but only nodded. "That's fine." Pulling a letter from her pocket, she handed it to Jeff.

"This came for Twilight and we picked it up with our mail." She pointed to the return address. "From the Washington State Department of Education, Mr. Smith-Jones. Must be the report of his visit. She'll be glad to get it. She's been curious as to what he'd say of her teaching methods."

Tommy was instantly enraged. "How could he say anything but good!"

His pride was evident and Jeff nodded. "I have to agree, Tom!" The man-to-man look they shared warmed Aunt Lucy. It was good for Tommy to know Jeff. He was more the age his own father would have been and while Jingles was the most wonderful grandpa in the world, still Tommy needed some of the experiences this young man could provide.

Twilight was thrilled with the letter. It actually turned out to be a copy of the report that had been turned in to the state after the spring visit to her classroom. It praised the spontaneous ability of "Miss Angel," even the nickname was included with the reason why, and mentioned that in all the curricula examined, taking into consideration methods, results, and test scores, none in the field of reading and arithmetic could be surpassed. It also wholeheartedly expressed the great pleasure and learning experience the end-of-school drama evening had given to the whole community and ended with highest compliments for Twilight. Copies were being forwarded to the local School Board and to her personnel file at the university.

Twilight couldn't believe it! To think she had been given such a tribute and from one who was in the position to evaluate!

"It makes me feel like I want to do even better this next year," she told Jeff humbly. "I hope I can live up to all the trust and faith expressed in that letter . . . and by my pupils and their parents," she added.

He took her seriously and replied, "That's why you've been given the tribute. So you can go forward and continue your work."

Twilight repeated the words to Jenny a few days later. Jenny agreed with Jeff.

"Have you ever noticed many times compliments or honors are given not only for past achievement but for potential? That's the way it should be, or we'd all think we'd arrived the minute someone praised us!" She paused and looked out the window at the darkening sky.

"Twilight, what if you hadn't come here? What if you'd never known any of the anger, fear, danger, that you've experienced in the past year? What if I hadn't been part of it all? We would still be the same two girls on the same tight little city schedule. Now —" She gestured to the scene before them.

"Do you know what I want to do? I want to go, take my nurse's training, become the best registered nurse that ever trained, then come back. Medical help is needed here, needed desperately. Just as you were able to help the children, I want to come back and help the community."

In spite of Twilight's instant leap of gladness she felt she had to point out, "It probably won't be easy."

Jenny looked at her oddly. "Nothing that's worthwhile ever is." Twilight was struck again with the knowledge that her little-girl sister was a woman, mature beyond her years in the things that really mattered. Her heart swelled with pride. What a service Jenny could give! She could think of no place else where she would be more useful. Without a word, she reached out to Jenny, caught her hand, and they stepped to the porch. Before them lay the evening, twilight time. Purple haze over the mountains heralded the approach of evening. Sleepy birds stilled their songs and the rustle of squirrels ceased. Side by side Twilight and Jenny stood on the porch of the little log cabin, thinking how much they had learned from Stehekin, thanking God for what it had meant in each of their lives.

One lone star peered through the violet haze, signaling for its companions to join its surveillance of the two girls on the porch — the two girls who had finally found their way through.

We hope you have enjoyed this Large Print book. Other Thorndike Press or Chivers Press Large Print books are available at your library or directly from the publishers.

For more information about current and upcoming titles, please call or write, without obligation, to:

Thorndike Press
P.O. Box 159
Thorndike, Maine 04986 USA
Tel. (800) 257-5157

OR

Chivers Press Limited
Windsor Bridge Road
Bath BA2 3AX
England
Tel. (0225) 335336

All our Large Print titles are designed for easy reading, and all our books are made to last.